SQUIBB.

Revenge!

by James David

Illustrated by James David

checked

To Helen...

First Published in the United Kingdom in 2008
by Moonbeam Publishing

ISBN 978-0954770464

Copyright © James David 2008

Bibliographical Data Services
British Library Cataloguing-in-Publication Data
A catalogue record for this book is available
from the British Library

Printed and bound by:
The Max Design & Print Co
Kettlestring Lane, Clifton Moor,
York YO30 4XF

what's
under
your
school?

MOONBEAM

Chapter 1

"Now, are you absolutely sure you'll be alright, all by yourself, son?" asked Maxwell's father, perched on the top step of the caravan, gazing up into the black, starry sky and clutching a slim glass of pineapple juice in his hand. "Supposin' you wake up in the middle of the night and panic...or have a spot of the *screamin' ab-dabs*!! I won't be around to hold your little mitt and give you a reassuring little hug!"

Maxwell, just inside the caravan, looked at his father from beneath his ginger fringe and wished he had the power to make him disappear...vanish into thin air...preferably skywards! Up to the stars he was gawping at! With an accompanying *whoosh*, he pictured his father zooming up into the blackness of the night as though he had a jet-pack strapped to his back! Or, perhaps some kind of giant vacuum cleaner nozzle would suddenly appear from nowhere and suck him up into the heavens!

'Let's face it,' thought Maxwell, 'had he *ever* woken up in the middle of the night, panicked

and had a spot of the *screamin' ab-dabs*?
No, never, and if he *did*, then his father would be the last person on the planet to come to his assistance!
He'd be too deep in the depths of *his own sleep*! So deep that even a bomb going off under his bed or a charging herd of elephants pouring out of his wardrobe wouldn't wake him!
No, he'd *never* be stirred by something as quiet as a spot of the *screamin' ab-dabs*!'

Mind you, his father *was* beginning to change...and change for the better!
That was all down to Rita!
To put you in the picture, things had certainly moved on since Christmas!
Maxwell's dad (Lenny) and Roberta's mum (Rita) had fallen head over heels for one another! The tango dancing had taken off in a big way and they spent hours upon hours every week practising in the Church Hall. Then, of course, there were the car-boots every Sunday from which they still managed to bring back home more junk between them than they ever sold! But at least Maxwell's dad's share was all crammed into a house now rather than into the caravan!
Yes, Lenny had moved in with Rita and they were both blissfully happy at No.34, Chestnut Terrace...and the pink and green caravan was now parked in the long grass in a corner of the field just behind the house!
"Dad, I'll be perfectly OK!" insisted Maxwell, wishing his father would get back to his sweetheart. "You know I've slept in this

blinkin' caravan *every night* for the last *six years*!!"
"Aye, but not by yourself!" suggested Mr Underdown after another sip of pineapple juice.

Maxwell glanced over his shoulder towards the narrow door that lead to his new bedroom at the end of the caravan. It was his dad's old room and he couldn't wait to stretch out on the big bed. For more than half his life he'd spent the nights on a narrow bunk-bed in the middle of the caravan opposite the little fire-place. Now, at least his feet would be nice and warm instead of sticking out beyond the blankets and turning into blocks of ice every night!

He looked back at his father who was now hovering over the bottom step.

"Right then, son, I'll leave you to it! And the best of luck!"

Why he should need luck Maxwell couldn't imagine!

Unless, of course, packs of marauding wolves or wild savages had been reported in this neck of Yorkshire, and his father was keeping quiet about them!

At last, Mr Underdown stepped into the field's damp, long grass and cast a look back at his son.

"Have a good night's sleep then, lad! And remember it's Sunday tomorrow, so Rita and me'll be car-bootin'. Are you comin' with us? I think Roberta'll be comin'!"

"I'll think about it!" mumbled Maxwell, glancing over at No.34. "I've got some homework to do for Miss Teezil. I might get on with that instead!"

Of course, he knew perfectly well that the wonderful Roberta wouldn't be going to the car-boot! She'd be coming over from the house to help him give the caravan a complete make-over!

They'd soon transform the place into the best den ever! In no time at all it would be perfectly perfect!

With the amount of junk doubling in No.34 when they'd moved in, there was hardly any room left for Maxwell! In fact he'd begun to feel like a bit of a spare part. In the way! Unwanted!

He reckoned his dad would have sold him if he'd been able to get a decent price...but who wants to buy a long, gawky, 'tall for his age' kid with an explosion of bright red hair at one end and a pair of enormous plates of meat (feet) at the other! There was just no demand at all for giant carrots, especially ones that needed feeding and clothing!

It seemed that the only person who appreciated his qualities was Roberta.

In an ideal world he would liked to have shared Robbie's room in the house, but it was soon made clear by the grown-ups that *that* particular idea was *definitely* out of the question!

It was then that he'd come up with his brainwave!

He volunteered to move out!

Into the caravan!

But on two conditions!

First, he must have the caravan completely, totally, utterly and exclusively to himself...and not as a place for dumping car-boot overflow, gardening tools or tins of paint!

Second, he could decorate it exactly how he liked...no adult interference at all! Not a hint of '*no, you can't do that!*', '*that's not a good idea!*' or '*oh no, son, we can't have that!*'

Amazingly, his dad had gladly agreed and even signed a contract drawn up by Robbie!

After all, thought Lenny to himself, Maxwell would not only be out of the way, but it would give him more room for all his junk...his present junk *and* his future junk! Perfect!

Mr Underdown even suggested rigging up an intercom to cover the short distance between No.34 and the caravan in the field just over the back fence.

Or even a mobile phone for Maxwell, so he could ring for emergency assistance in case of a spot of the '*screamin' ab-dabs*' or, even worse, an attack of the '*eebie-jeebies*'!

Maxwell's ears had certainly pricked up at that idea!

Not the idea of keeping in touch with his father, you understand!

More like the idea of being able to keep in touch with the wonderful Roberta!

Since Christmas, the two of them had become the best of friends and were just about inseparable. They could hardly wait to change the caravan into a den so they could spend time together under a different roof from the grown-up love-birds of No.34.

Mr Underdown drained the last drops of pineapple juice from his glass.

"Sleep well then!" he called as he marched off through the grass towards Chestnut Terrace.

'*At last*!!' thought Maxwell.

"See you tomorrow!" he replied, as politely as he could. "Sleep well, too!"

He closed the caravan door and slid the bolt.

'*At last, the place to m'self*!' he thought.

He looked around the only home he had known for the last six years. It seemed so empty without all the car-boot junk. All that space was hiding there after all, drowned for years and years with every sort of rubbish you could imagine. It now seemed so spacious.

So much room!

It had turned into a little palace!

And it was *all* his!

And Robbie's, of course!

At the opposite end from the bedroom was a three-sided square of long cushions surrounding a small table. Above them were storage cupboards and gas-mantle lamps. Along one of the side walls was another cupboard, a tall one like a narrow wardrobe. Next to that was his old bunk bed. Opposite was a little gas-fire with its tiny mantel-shelf, a sink with a pocket-handkerchief draining-board and a small gas-stove with two rusty old rings. Between that and the door was another tall cupboard.

Or rather it *looked* like a cupboard! Actually it held the chemical loo!

It was so cramped that when you were sitting on it, your knees stopped you from shutting the door!

Maxwell walked over to the mantel-shelf and looked at the only decoration in the whole caravan. It was his greatest treasure! A crumpled old photograph of him aged about four, his father and, most importantly, his mother, Meg...on a holiday in Clacton.

They were on the beach and looked great together, like a real family. All happy and smiley! But it was only a few short weeks after that wonderful holiday that Maxwell's mum had been tragically killed by a drunk driver.

And that had been that! Normal, happy family life over in a split second.

But now, after nearly seven long years of moving around the country in the pink and green Morris Minor and the matching caravan...perhaps his dad might just settle down again...and family life might resume!

He looked through the little window above his old bed and glanced over at the dark shape of the houses of Chestnut Terrace.

No.34 was the future, he hoped. He crossed his fingers and made a silent wish. Then he closed the curtains, sat down on the edge of his old bunk and thought about what would be happening on Sunday.

A smile beamed across his face, almost from ear to ear!

He couldn't wait!

Chapter 2

Maxwell had already decided how he wanted his new home decorated. He wanted jungle, pure jungle! All in celebration of the *'waking-up dream'* that he and Roberta shared. It was one of the things that had drawn them together before Christmas, when Maxwell had started at *Chestnut Hill Juniors.* It seemed really strange! Both of them always had the exact same dream just before they woke up every morning! A dream full of screeching parrots, chattering

chimpanzees and tropical trees...and they were always swinging through the jungle on long, drooping creepers and ropes, getting closer and closer to a great, deep, uncrossable valley...and that's where the dream ended, every single day! They'd never got across the valley once between them!

They'd also discovered other things they had in common, too. They were both *'only children'* with no brothers or sisters. They both had *'single parents'* (Maxwell thought they should be called *'only parents'*!) who were crazy about the same hobbies: tango dancing and collecting junk!

And they both had lost parents who had died. Robbie's dad had been killed in an explosion at his works three years ago when she was seven. It had happened just before Christmas which had made it even worse.

Maxwell walked over to what he called the 'sitting room' at the end of the caravan...the bit with the table surrounded by long cushions on three sides. He reached up into one

of the food cupboards and grabbed a bag of crisps and a can of dandelion and burdock, his favourite drink. He was just about to sit down at the table and get stuck into his homework...when he was suddenly stopped in his tracks!

What was that?

A noise!

He listened intently, frozen in mid-action like a statue, crisps in one hand and the can in the other.

Then he heard the same noise again!

A sort of muffled thud!

And it was coming from *underneath the caravan*!

In slow motion, his heart beginning to race, he put the crisps and can on the table and tip-toed towards the little gas-fire. That's where the noise seemed to have come from.

He stood perfectly still and listened.

What on earth could it have been?

Then a third thud, a louder one, exploded into the quietness of the caravan, this time from straight beneath his feet!

The floor even shook!

Some*one or* some*thing* was banging on the caravan floor!

Maxwell's heart began to beat even faster, and, to be honest, he was beginning to feel a little scar...

Then another bang rattled the floor!

He even felt his feet shake!

Fear began to sweep through him!

He couldn't believe it!

He'd been left in his own little palace for no more than five minutes and he was about to have a spot of the *'screamin' ab-dabs'* or, even worse, an attack of the *'eebie-jeebies'*!

His father had been right after all!

It's what he'd predicted!

And it had happened within five minutes!

He could hear his dad's *'told you so!'* digs ringing in his ears!

Or, even worse, his *'are you a man or a mouse?'* jibes!

He'd be scoffing his head off for the next twelve months if he found out about this one!

No, he had to stand firm, control himself!

He had to take charge of the situation!

After all, it was *only* some kind of subterranean monster trying to get at him! A monster that had sensed food above ground! The crisps perhaps! Or *him*!

A giant mole that had been sleeping underground for thousands of years had suddenly awoken!

It was starving and on the rampage...

Thud!

The noise exploded again from under his feet!

Then...with his pulse beating in his ears and beads of sweat breaking out on his freckly forehead...

...he heard another sound...

...a faint human voice...

"Help!...I'm stuck under 'ere!! Help!!"

A look of puzzled bewilderment arranged itself on Maxwell's face. The look of stricken horror was suddenly replaced by one of surprised wonder!

"It was *Roberta*!"

But what was she doing out at this time of night and what on earth was she doing *under the caravan*?

Maxwell quickly composed himself, grabbed his torch, darted to the door and slid back the bolt. In a flash he was on his knees in the damp grass, shining the torchbeam under the caravan.

A moment later, it fell upon Robbie, lying almost flat and all curled up, supporting her head off the ground with her hand and elbow. The torchbeam lit her face a ghostly white.

"You're dazzling me!" she squinted.

Maxwell looked at her and put his fingers over the torch to cut down the light.

"Is that you? Robbie?" he mumbled.

"Of course it's me! Who do you think it is? Father Christmas?"

Maxwell again looked puzzled.

"You look different, that's all!"

"You'll look different when I get hold of you! Are you going to rescue me or keep staring at me as though you've just discovered a long lost mummy in an Egyptian tomb? I'm stuck by my hair! I've got it caught up in some greasy nuts and bolts under here!"

"But what're you doing under there in the first place?"

"Look, Edward Maxwell Underdown, if you don't stop asking questions and get me out of here...!"

Maxwell wriggled under his new home and carefully unknotted Robbie's hair from the grimy metalwork.

"It's all different! Your hair!" he gasped, as he strained to free his best mate.

"I know! I've just done it! It's great! Just wait until you see it!" enthused Roberta, relieved at last that her gallant knight-in-shining-armour was rescuing her from being trapped in the nasty duke's dark, dank cellar!

A few moments later they were both squirming out from beneath the caravan into the open air.

"Well, are you going to invite me in? I've been stuck under there since I saw your dad coming over with his pineapple juice! I'm supposed to be doing Miss Teezil's homework in m'bedroom but I couldn't resist coming over and being your first visitor! That's when I saw your dad coming behind me, so I quickly hid under the caravan...and listened to him wittering on for ages! Going on about you having the '*screamin' ab-jabs*' because you're here all by yourself! What does he think you are? A *man or a mouse*?"

Maxwell gulped and said nothing. He pushed the

door open and waved Robbie in. He shut the door behind her and stared again at his best mate.

"Wow! You certainly look different!"

"What do you think? Good or bad?"

"Well, it'll take some gettin' used to...but first impressions...not bad!"

"Not bad? Is that all you can say, after all that work this afternoon?"

Apparently, because her first attempts at drawing up legal contracts had worked for Maxwell and his caravan, she'd had a go at producing another! This time between herself and her mother!

For years she'd wanted to change her hair. It had always been long and straight and blonde. Everytime she'd wanted it cut and a different colour, the answer from Rita had been a definite no-no!

But now, amazingly, because Maxwell had got his way with the caravan, Rita had softened a touch.

Perhaps it was the Lenny factor!

Him being in her life and all that...and Mrs Nudd being a lot happier as a result. Robbie didn't know, but, whatever the reason...she was going to get something out of it for herself!

And it had worked! Rita had signed on the dotted line!

In return for helping on car-boot Sundays for one whole year without a trace of a single moan...she could do what she liked with her hair...and her mum wouldn't say a word! She could shave the lot off if she wanted!

"Do you want a *dan 'n bur*?" asked Maxwell, still sort of addressing Robbie's hairstyle rather then Robbie herself.

She nodded and looked at Maxwell's mop of untidy, unbrushed ginger hair.

"You could do the same! Give that lot a make-over!"

Maxwell shook his head as he reached up for another can.

"No chance, mate! This caravan make-over is quite enough to be going on with for the time being. 'Sides, I quite like m' mop! It's *distinctive*! No one else has got *anything* like this upstairs!"

"You mean the *bird's nest* look!" laughed Robbie.

"Or the *natural mop* look! That's it...the *natch thatch*!"

Roberta grabbed her drink and looked at her

reflection in the sitting room window. In the soft light of the glowing gas-mantles, her hair now was certainly *distinctive*, too. The long, blonde had gone to be replaced by short-cropped bright green, gelled up into a forest of spikes...one or two of them now tipped with black grease from under the caravan!

"You look like you've got a fluorescent hedgehog perched on your head!" joked Maxwell, standing next to Roberta and bending his knees so their hair-do's were almost level in the window.

"Well, I did it to celebrate our jungle den!" said Robbie. "By the end of tomorrow it will be all green, and leafy and foresty...like me! I can't wait to start! What time do you want me over here with all the stuff I've collected?"

"As soon as you can! I guess you've got to honour your contract with your mum and help her set up the car-boot stall without a single moan!"

Robbie nodded and drained her can of dandelion and burdock.

"I reckon I'll be here by nine-ish! OK? And I'll bring some grub so we can have a picnic! And don't forget, at sometime tomorrow we've got to feed the squibbitz at school and give then some exercise!"

While Maxwell was still at half-mast she pecked him on the cheek. He slightly blushed as usual, but secretly he quite liked Robbie's little signs of affection. He'd never had a girl-friend before, but he really enjoyed her company, ever since they'd met on Maxwell's first day at *Chestnut Hill Juniors* just before Christmas. The day they'd both sat on the '*Crack*' down the middle of the hall...and the day they'd bravely taken on the enemy...Grimmage and Grubbage...and discovered their little secret!

Maxwell gave Roberta a peck on the cheek in return.

"Right, I'd better be off then!" smiled Robbie. "Or I'll be miss..."

She suddenly stopped and the smile on her face instantly vanished.

They'd both noticed it.

Through the window, beyond their reflections.

A light.

A moving beam of light.

Bouncing in the darkness that surrounded the little caravan.

Someone was out there!

Chapter 3

Maxwell quickly grabbed, twisted and pushed the door handle, nearly ripping the narrow door off its hinges.

"There, heading to the corner of the field!" he shouted, pointing to a tall, fleeing shape of gangly arms and even more gangly legs, vanishing into the night.

"Who on earth was *that*?" gasped Robbie, a touch nervously, looking around in the dark to see if there was anyone else.

"I'm pretty sure it was just the *one* guy!" said Maxwell. "But, boy oh boy, could he *move*! He must have legs like a giraffe! He was across the field like greased lightning!"

"But what was he doing?" wondered Roberta. "He certainly wasn't out for a little night-time walkies with his pooch! That's for sure!" She looked up at Maxwell and slid her hand into his.

"Are you sure you're going to be OK?" she quietly asked.

"Oh no! Don't *you* start! M'pa was bad enough. Not *you* as w...!"

"Hang on, what's *that*?" burst Roberta, gazing down into the long grass just beyond the caravan steps.

"Look, there's a feather...a *parrot's* feather!"

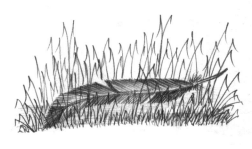

Maxwell jumped down and picked it up gently with both hands as though it was made of the finest, most fragile crystal glass.

The beautiful, sleek red and yellow feather, about the length of a ruler, sat across his hands and looked magnificent. Certainly not the sort of thing you see every day...especially in a field behind a row of terraced houses in the Yorkshire town of Kirkthwaite!

"That's peculiar!" he mumbled, as the feather twitched in the slight breeze. "Did that guy drop it? Was he snooping around the caravan, spying on us? And...even worse...!"

He stopped and looked up at Roberta with a serious look on his face. "There's only *one* place this feather could have come from!" he said.

"And we both know where *that* is!" whispered Roberta.

"Come on!" said Maxwell decisively. "We've got to check that everything's OK at school! Something could have happened to *you know what*!!"

And with that, the two intrepid adventurers sped into the night, guided only by the light of Maxwell's trusty torch. What they would find at Chestnut Hill at just after ten o'clock on a Saturday night in April was anybody's guess...but what they *did* discover would leave them both shaken and chilled to the bone! Indeed...it was to be a sight that...

...they would...*never...ever...forget*!!

Meanwhile, somewhere in the middle of nowhere, in the midst of the bleak, fog-cloaked moorlands that

separate the counties of Yorkshire and Lancashire in the North of England... a dozen flickering candle flames danced crazily in the damp wind that slithered and whined over the boggy heather where sensible people never ventured.

In this particular place in the middle of nowhere, the wicked wind, that occasionally raged and howled, had crept under the doors and through the cracks in the walls of an ancient, ruined hexagonal tower that had all but crumbled to nothing. It had long been called *Murkbog Towers*. Only two rooms remained to take on the eternal wind. One above the other, joined by a spiral staircase. The lower room had a heavy oaken door that held back the elements as well as it could, while the upper room's boarded up windows were no match at all against the slithering, whining wind that hungrily wrapped itself around its crumbling, helpless, stony prey.

And it was in the lower room, that the twelve candle flames flickered and danced in the chill, damp, swirling draught.

Eight were gathered in a rusted, curly iron candelabra that dangled and swayed from the ceiling. The other four were in brass, barley-twist candle sticks that sat in the middle of the large, round, rough wooden table that dominated the stone-flagged floor. Other than the table, there was hardly any more furniture in the room. Just three ornately carved chairs with threadbare, blue velvet seats kept the table company.

Where the floor met one of the six walls a sizeable stone fireplace with a bare mantel-shelf sheltered the glowing embers of a fire. The wind tended the ashes so they never faded and died, waiting for the room's inhabitants to return and poke them into life and feed them with dry wood.

Scattered around the stone floor were a variety of old pots and pans and at the foot of the walls on either side of the fireplace were two untidy piles of sheets and blankets. Nearby was a dog-eared cardboard box half full of tinned food, a brown, stained, plastic washing-up bowl and a large, green, rusty, metal water-container.

It seemed that the grim cell was definitely the draughty, dismal home of two luckless souls.

Indeed, the room was home for a certain, cowardly couple of rogues. A particularly prickly pair of villains who had been driven out of the town beyond the moors, and taken shelter in the ruined tower.

The diabolical, dastardly duo of rascals who had run Chestnut School with iron fists and whiplash tongues for years and years.

The tremendously, terrible twosome of scoundrels who had plotted and planned to make a fortune by cruelly exploiting a hundred innocent creatures!

I think by now you probably know the identity of the couple of rogues in question. So the less said about them the better!

All I will say is that at the very same moment as Maxwell and Roberta were galloping across the field following the torchbeam, their clapped out old car was just making its bumpy, wind-buffeted way along the potholed moorland track that led to their desperate, stony shelter.

The twelve flickering candle flames continued to crazily dance in the damp, swirling air of the lower room, ready to reluctantly welcome their gruesome guests and eavesdrop upon their latest, devilish plots and sly schemes.

There had, in recent days, been much talk around the wooden table of pay-back time and revenge.

And the moment had now arrived for action!

The *squibbitz* would soon be back with their rightful owners!

Fortune making could begin again!!

Unfortunately, the listening flickering candle flames had no means by which to warn the world beyond

16

the moors of what was about to happen.

If they could have done...it would all have been a different story.

A very different story indeed!

Maxwell and Robbie reached the gate at the other side of the field and Maxwell switched off his torch. They looked up and down the road. There were no signs at all of the fleeing stranger.

"Vanished into thin air!" sighed Robbie. "I wonder who he was!"

"I haven't a clue," whispered Maxwell, "but we're gonna have to be on our guard in case he's a spy for the old enemy. He could be crouching behind this hedge right now, for instance! At this very second! Listening to our every single word, with all sorts of spy-like, James Bond listening gadgets!"

He imagined a super sleuth on their trail, hidden in the bushes, tuning in to some kind of state-of-the-art bugging device.

Then he beckoned to Robbie with a finger across his lips.

"Sshh! No more words for the time being!" he whispered.

Roberta motioned '*follow me*!' with a wave of her arm, and the two of them dashed along the road, now guided by street lamps.

Soon they were at the school-gates. They were locked as usual for the weekend, but it was still easy to climb over the iron railings. Softly they both landed like cats on the tarmac of the playground and headed for their *special* door.

Since Christmas, when Miss Teezil had taken over as Headteacher of Chestnut Hill, all the locks had been changed and all the windows strengthened with metal mesh. Not to keep out local vandals, yobs and thieves, you understand! But to keep out the likes of the former headmonster, the loathesome, reptilian Grimmage and his side-kick and collaborator, the former school-cook and concoctor of foul school-dinners, Grubbage!

The squibbitz had to be protected from them!

There was always the suspicion and worry that they might just try and grab them all, and still make their fame and fortune!

The fabulous animals now lived in the school-house, once occupied by Grimmage. It was next door to the school to which it was linked by a door at the back of the hall stage. If you remember they used to live in cramped cages beneath the school, but Maxwell and Roberta had moved them to more spacious accommodation, with, of course, Miss Teezil's consent. She continued to live in her small terraced house in a street near the school, and she was quite happy to do so! She had no intention of living in Grubbage's old house with its one enormous room, its water-pump and its huge chestnut tree! Wading about knee deep in brown, crinkly leaves would have driven her mad!

So far, and it was now nearly Easter, there had been no sign at all of Grimmage and Grubbage. Since the day they had driven away in the snow watched by millions of world-wide television viewers and the fuming and frozen mega-star of stage and screen, Miss Leonora Divine, no one had seen nor heard a single sign of the scoundrels.

But defences had to be kept up!

They could strike at any moment!

Roberta reached for the secret key. It was hidden wedged in a crack between two loose stones in the classroom wall behind one of the giant plantpots which adorned the *new* playground. During the Spring term all sorts of decorations had been added to the bleak, boring patch of black tarmac that Grimmage had insisted upon. There were big, bushy plants in pots, flower tubs, a giant chess-set, hop-scotch grids, climbing frames, a slide, netball posts, a football goal...and in one corner a large hole was being excavated to become a future wildlife pond!

Things had certainly changed!

Robbie grabbed the key and opened the classroom door.

They stepped inside and Maxwell switched his torch back on, keeping his fingers across the front so as not to let out too much light. The last thing they wanted was one of the school neighbours ringing the police to report a break-in!

Not a sound could be heard as they tiptoed across the

classroom between the rows of desks. It was Miss Teezil's classroom, of course. Now a riot of colour compared to the old days, when Grimmage demanded that there was no art, and walls must remain blank and grey. Her pupils' artwork was everywhere, together with their handwritten stories, picture displays, shelves and shelves of interesting books and board-games and a giant nature table crammed with things to look at and examine. There was even a small theatre in the corner with curtains that opened and closed, for the children to perform their plays.

In another corner was an old electric oven for baking and cookery lessons!

And, believe it or not...there wasn't a single computer!

There hadn't been any in Grimmage's time either.

It was one thing Miss Teezil and her predecessor actually agreed on! They both reckoned that keyboards and computer screens were totally unnecessary for learning at junior school!

They were banned! There was so much else to do...and so little time to do it!

And the result was that all her children just loved being at school! So much so that they were genuinely unwilling to go home at the end of each day! They were disappointed when she said, "Time to pack your things away! It's three-thirty!" She almost had to prise her pupils out of their wonderfully old-fashioned wooden desks with their squeaky lids.

They regarded them as their 'other' homes, with pictures decorating their insides and other personal bits and pieces. They even polished the desks on Fridays with real furniture polish!

Maxwell and Roberta crept past the huge, long blackboard (no whiteboards here!) with its long narrow ledge littered with dozens of bits of coloured chalk, white chalk and board-rubbers. Quietly, they opened the classroom door and stole into the corridor. Spooky silver moonshine and shadows were eerily scattered across the floor and walls.

They both gazed down towards the dark hall doors.

And it was then...that they saw it!

Their hearts raced, the hairs stood up on the backs of their necks and flushes of goosebumps sprung up on their arms!

They both shivered and looked at one another.

There was a strange light creeping under the hall doors and through their little windows.

And it wasn't a calm, still light.

It was moving.

Jerking and darting around, changing colour from white, to blue, to green, to orange, to red and back again.

Was someone in the hall?

Was it the fleeing stranger from the field?

Or was it someone else?

Maxwell grabbed hold of Roberta's hand...

...and together they crept forward into the unknown...

Chapter 4

As the clapped-out old car spluttered to a halt in the middle of a huge, grassy puddle outside *Murkbog Towers*, Mrs Grubbage angrily pushed her door wide open. Her great supersize wellies slowly swung out and sank with a great splash into the soggy bog.

"Bog by name and bog by nature!" she grumbled. "If only you'd park just over there, I could step out onto terra firma instead of up to m'knees in bog water everytime we come back to this God forsaken dump!"

"Ssstop croaking, you old hag!" snapped back Grimmage. "And help me with the box of sssupplies. Think yourself lucky that you've got a roof over your head and a place to kip!"

They both paddled and sloshed around to the back of the car, opened the boot and struggled in the wind to lift the enormous box piled high with all the groceries for the week ahead.

"Luck? You must be joking!" gasped Mrs Grubbage, as she fought to grab hold of the corners of the box. "To start with, the place has only *just* got a roof. The next great storm...and capput...that'll be that! And, if you think I've had any kip at all since we've been here, then you can think again! What, with the drippin' roof, the howlin' wind and you snoring your head off!"

"One last heave and she'll be out!" panted Grimmage, awkwardly grasping the other end of the box in his bony talons.

Slowly but surely, the great box glided out of the boot.

"Now, you, Mrs Grubbage, takin' your time, walk slowly backwards onto dry land." instructed Grimmage. "We'll have this lot in Murkbog in next to no time!"

Mrs Grubbage, biting her bottom lip and grasping her end of the box as tightly as she could, took one and then two sploshy steps backwards. Grimmage followed.

Splish! Splash! Splish! Splash!

Everything seemed to be going well.

They'd soon be in the dry and warm.

They could get the fire blazing, put the kettle on...

...and have a nice, refreshing cup of...

But then...double disaster struck!

Mrs Grubbage took her next step backwards...and suddenly, her whole, rather ample body slumped and lurched down to one side! Her right wellie had plunged into a hidden, deep abyss in the giant puddle.

"Get up, woman!" exclaimed Grimmage. "Straighten up, you old bat! The whole lot's going to tip over into the drink!"

"I can't, I can't, it's got me!" screamed Mrs Grubbage. "The bog's got me! I'm sinkin'! It's pullin' me down!"

Then, at exactly the same time, a wicked gust of wind saw a chance for fun.

It wrapped itself with glee around the stranded pair and the lop-sided box.

The box wobbled even more...then both Grimmage and Grubbage lost their balance...and the whole sorry trio plunged into the mire with an enormous splash!

The cardboard box had completely flipped over.

Food was everywhere, floating and sinking into the bog.

Grimmage and Grubbage flapped around like demented sea-lions, eventually emerging from the murky waters, with dripping, mud streaked faces, their heads draped with a nice mixture of weeds, slices of bacon, frog spawn and soggy, pink toilet paper.

Grimmage glared at Grubbage, seething through his muddy lips. "Mark my wordsss, you old witch!" he hissed, with a shiver, "I'll...have...your...gutsss...for gartersss!!"

At the very same moment, back in civilisation on the outskirts of Kirkthwaite...at No.34, Chestnut Terrace to be precise...Mrs Nudd was taking a bedtime glass of milk upstairs to her daughter's bedroom. Vases of plastic flowers stood on every single flowery carpeted step. The rose covered wallpaper together with the wafting rose scent was almost overpowering. But Mrs Nudd loved it.

She was flower crazy! Not to mention *tango crazy* as well, as the Latin American rhythms filled the air from the record player in the hall. She reached the top of the stairs, turned right and gently tapped on Roberta's bedroom door. Her body never stopped moving as it wove around to the music. It was as though she was dancing with the glass of milk!

There was no answer!

'Must have dropped off to sleep doing her homework! Bless!' she thought, with a smile.

She pushed the door open and peeped inside.

There wasn't a sign of her daughter.

"Robbie, where are you?" she called.

No answer.

She put the glass of milk on top of the chest of drawers by the door and checked the loo.

Still no sign.

"Lenny!" she called downstairs, through the rose-garden.

Mr Underdown appeared in the hall, jigging to the music, as though he had an invasion of ants in his pants. He was firmly grasping another slim glass of pineapple juice.

"What's up, luv?"

"Our Robbie's not down there is she? She's not up here!"

"She'll be havin' a sneaky bite to eat in t' kitchen, I bet! Her stomach's like a bottomless pit on Saturdays!"

He quickly shuffled and sashayed down the hall towards the kitchen as though he was on a dance-floor, dancing with his fruit juice.

"No, no sign of her here!" he called back, marching up to the record-player and turning the volume down.

"Rob-er-ta, where are you?" he called.

Mrs Nudd echoed him upstairs.

There was still no answer.

"I bet she's gone over to that caravan of yours!" Rita complained as she grabbed the glass of milk and made her way downstairs. "The number of times we've told her...*let us know if you're going over there, especially at night*...you don't know who's lurkin' about!"

Lenny reached for his jacket that was hanging on one of the coat pegs in the hall.

"I'll be back in a couple of secs!" he smiled. "I'll make a face at the window and scare 'em to death! Last time I caught 'em canoodlin'!

You should have seen Maxwell! His face was a picture! It turned the colour of them roses on your wallpaper, in one second flat!"

"Well, I hope you're right!" said Rita anxiously. "I don't know what we'll do if she's not there either. But I'll tell you this, Lenny Underdown.

If she's not there, then she's definitely for the high jump when she *does* get in! You just wait until I get m' hands on the young madam!"

Chapter 5

Hand in hand, Maxwell and Roberta crept nervously closer and closer to the hall doors, their eyes fixed on the strange, mesmerising lights.

It was as quiet as a graveyard.

All they could hear were their own heartbeats thumping away in their ears.

They tip-toed closer and closer.

Should they go on...or turn back?

What *were* they going to find in the school hall at getting on for *eleven o'clock on a Saturday night*?

They were definitely beginning to have second thoughts.

Maxwell unknowingly gripped Roberta's hand even tighter.

The pain made her scream a silent scream and pull a face that in itself made Maxwell wince with horror. He quickly let go of her hand, and Robbie gratefully shook it.

"Sorry!" he whispered, beads of sweat budding on his forehead.

"Anyone would think you were scared!!" Robbie whispered back, with a grin.

"I am!" Maxwell mouthed, the words failing to come out.

Roberta grabbed hold of Maxwell's hand this time and beckoned him forward. She seemed absolutely fearless.

Five seconds later, they were almost within touching distance of the two doors. Slowly, they moved their heads forwards and peeped through the two little windows...and what they saw made them gasp with amazement!

Suddenly, at No.34, the front door burst open and Mr Underdown charged in as though his trousers were on fire!
"Rita! Rita!" he bellowed down the hallway. "There's no sign of either of 'em at the caravan! They've *both* vanished!"
Rita appeared from the kitchen, her face ashen and etched with worry.
"Then we've got to call the police, Lenny!" she said as calmly as she could. "There's nothing else we can do!"
"You do that, luv!" agreed Lenny. "And I'll keep searchin'!"
He scrabbled about in one of the many boxes of car-boot junk in the hall and grabbed a torch. He switched it on to see if it worked. Nothing. He tried another. Still nothing. The third one worked.
"I'll be back as soon as I've found 'em!" he called. " And don't worry, luv, they'll turn up! I don't know about my Maxwell, but your Roberta's got a good 'ead on her shoulders! She's a little princess!"
As he dashed back out into the night, Mrs Nudd instantly broke down and began to sob. Hearing the words '*little princess*' hadn't helped! And she knew in her heart of hearts that something nasty would happen as soon as her 'precious little girl' changed her beautiful, long blonde hair for that horrible, teenage, spiky, green mess she now wore on the top of her head! If only she hadn't listened to her daughter's silly demands and signed her silly contract!
Still sobbing, and thinking she'd lost her daughter in more ways than one, she tried to find her mobile phone amongst the heaps of even more car-boot junk that filled the front room. She was becoming more and more angry. Not with Roberta, but with herself. She'd *never* forgive herself if anything happened.
And, of course, as she frantically tried to find the mobile phone, her imagination began to get the better of her. Every possible nightmare flashed through her mind, and her anger with herself began to build and build. She even regretted meeting Lenny, cursing the day they'd met at the car-boot before Christmas. She should never have suggested he move in with her! And what a crazy idea it was to let

young Maxwell stay in the caravan in the field behind the house! It was a ridiculous idea! He wasn't safe over there! And neither was her little princess!

She sat down on the settee and wept even more.

Fortunately, as she plucked a paper tissue from a box on a pile of old black records belonging to Lenny, she spotted the phone sticking out from beneath a flowery cushion.

She switched it on, and through the tears, she managed, with a shaking finger, to press the number nine button three times.

Meanwhile, at Murkbog Towers, a steamy mist wisped upwards into the damp, cool draughty air. The two scoundrels, Grimmage and Grubbage, shivering in their wet clothing, sat by a roaring fire. Each was nibbling a dry cream-cracker and sipping from a mug of cold water from the green, rusty can.

"Not even a single tea-bag to have a cup of tea!" grumbled Grubbage.

"And there's hardly a crumb left to eat. We *needed* those supplies!"

"Well if *you* want to go diving in that bog outside, you're welcome!" snapped Grimmage from the other side of the fireplace. "I'm sure we can dry out some of that *lovely* bacon, or those *delicious* sausages, or that *scrumptious* sherry trifle! All you had to do was walk backwards across the blithering bog! And you couldn't even manage that, you clumsy old hag!"

"How was I to know there was a great, whopping hole for me to plunge into?" Grubbage argued. "If only you'd parked the car exactly where I'd told you in the first place, none of this would have happened, and we'd be tuckin' in to a feast by now!"

"Just keep your fingers crossed that our good friend, T.G., brings something to get our gnashers round!" hissed Grimmage. "The man'll be here in a few minutes. Let's hope everything's gone to plan and he's done his nasty little deed at that festering, little blister of a school we used to run!"

"And he's managed to find out where that little nuisance of an urchin lives!" added Grubbage, with a wild look in her eye. "That evil, plotting, lanky carrot of a child...a certain Master Edward Maxwell Underdown...!"

Grimmage crunched hard on his dry cream-cracker and gazed into the fire.

"Revenge will be sssso ssssweet!" he hissed, as the twelve flickering candle-flames continued their dance, along with the ghostly shadows that criss-crossed the cold, stone-flagged floor.

"Revenge will be sssso ssssweet!"

At Chestnut Hill School, the two intrepid adventurers could hardly believe their eyes, as they stared through the little windows of the hall doors.

All the curtains were closed. Even the huge stage-curtains were drawn together. Two widening beams of light cut through the

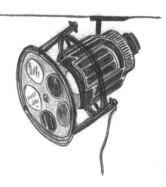

darkness... one green and one red. They were coming from the two spotlights which Grimmage had fixed on the ceiling years ago. The ones he used to move about with a remote-control. One beam produced a large circle of green on the stage-curtains and the other a smaller red oval on the floorboards. Suddenly the colours changed to orange and white.

Maxwell shoved his face onto the little glass window and peered up at the ceiling.

"There's...like discs...with transparent circles of colour in front of each light...," he gasped, "and they're slowly movin' round by 'em selves!"

"It's like some kind of weird disco!" Robbie whispered. "But there's no people, and no music!"

"But who could have set it all up?" wondered Maxwell. "Surely not Miss Teezil?"

Suddenly, the colours changed again.

This time to red and blue.

The children's eyes widened as they gazed at the two great shapes of light.

Their mouths slowly opened with shock.

The same enormous words were written in scrawling, spooky printing across each dazzling patch.

The words *'Revenge is Sweet!'*

Roberta pushed open the hall doors and stepped into the glowing hall. Her face blushed purply maroon in the light as she beckoned Maxwell to follow.

They watched the slowly revolving discs above them as the colours changed again. The stage-curtains now had a white circle, and the floor became green...but the words had vanished.

"The words must keep coming up every few changes!" whispered Maxwell. "But who could have...?"

Suddenly, a blood-curdling squawk filled the eerie green hall.

The heads of Maxwell and Roberta sprung around as though they were on springs.

And there, in the back corner of the hall...they could see two tall, cylindrical cages standing next to one another on the floor...each with a brightly coloured parrot sat on a perch. Sawdust and feathers were scattered on the floorboards just beyond the bars of each cage.

Then they saw, between them and the two parrots, a strange machine sitting at the foot of the hall's back wall. It was like some sort of projector combined with a large, old fashioned tape-recorder.

Maxwell and Roberta stood frozen to the spot.

It was all so peculiar.

What was going on in the hall?

Who had set it all up, and *how* had they got in to the school?

One of the parrots suddenly squawked again as the colours in the hall changed. This time to blue and orange.

And then, the parrots spoke, one after the other.

In chilling voices that sent shivers dancing up and down the spines of the two children. They knew *exactly* who had taught them the words. "Presssss the red button!" said one.

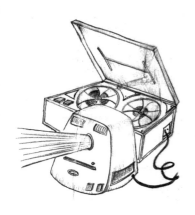

"Presssss the green!" said the other.

As the colours in the hall slowly changed to green and red, Maxwell and Roberta, as though under some magical spell walked towards the strange contraption.

"It's electrical." whispered Maxwell. "Look, there's wires all over the place!"

"There's even wires stretching up to the spotlights!" pointed Robbie.

"Everything's all connected! And I think we know who's behind it all, don't we? That voice was unmistakable! He's trained these birds like he trained the ten parrots that taught the squibbitz to speak!"

"But surely Grimmage can't have set *all* this up *by himself*!" said Maxwell. "And why's he done it? Why's he gone to all this trouble?"

"To scare everyone on Monday," replied Robbie. "To show that he's back and means business!"

The colours changed again to orange and white.

"Do you think we ought to press the buttons?" asked Maxwell.

"I do!" insisted Roberta. "To see if he gives any clues about what he's going to do to get the squibbitz back! And then we ought to dismantle the whole lot, get rid of it and keep it all a secret. Not even Miss Teezil must know!"

As Roberta's fingers found the buttons on the machine, the colours changed again...to red and blue...and with them the terrifying words re-appeared, scrawled on the stage-curtains and across the floorboards.

'Revenge is Sweet!'

All glowed purply maroon again.

Her fingers hovered over the red and green buttons.

She looked nervously into Maxwell's eyes...

...and pressed!!

With a couple of clicks and a high-pitched buzz,

Chapter 6

the strange, electrical contraption sprung into action!
First, the giant, plastic reels of recording tape began to revolve, and
then a brilliantly white beam of light
shot across the hall from back to
front, totally erasing the colours from
the two spotlights. The red stage-
curtains became a glowing, pink
cinema screen, wrinkled by all the
vertical folds and creases.

Then, from speakers hidden
somewhere behind the curtains, a
loud crackling hiss filled the hall and
then huge black, jerky numbers began
to flicker onto the screen, counting
quickly down from *10*...to *5*...to *3, 2, 1*...
And then...to the horror of the two secret viewers...the enormous face
of Grimmage filled the screen from top to bottom!
Maxwell and Roberta cowered at the sight before them in all its
disgustingly lurid colours.
There he was, his head hundreds of times its real size...viciously

staring at them from the front of the hall! Every detail of the horrific face was there, *but magnified a hundred times*!

The warty, beaked nose...the bulbous, bloodshot eyes...the nasty brown dribbles dripping from that reptilian mouth...the floppy fungus ears... the bushy, bird-wing eyebrows...and that crinkled, totally bald head!

It was the most grizzly, ghastly and gruesome sight they had ever seen in their lives. So much so that they shielded their eyes from the monstrously hideous and repulsive sight with their hands, just squinting through gaps between their fingers.

But then...things became even worse!

The foul image began to move!

The mouth opened to reveal two gappy rows of brown and green teeth, and a slimy tongue that whipped in and out like a snake's!

Then the eyes slowly winked, one after the other, like some great, fat lizard's!

And then...*what could be worse*?

The monster began to *speak*!

It was like being back in school-assembly before Christmas...but a thousand times worse!

Maxwell and Roberta wanted to cover their ears, but the sound was so loud, the words they heard burrowed their way into their heads so deeply that they would never, ever forget them. The horror was almost complete!

> *"Greetingsss, ssstaff and pupilsss of*
> *Chessstnut Hill Ssschool!*
> *Your headmonsssster isss back!*
> *He isss after...REVENGE!*
> *And be warned!*
> *He will get it!*
> *And have ALL your GUTSSS...*
> *for GARTERSSS!!!"*

The sound stopped, the picture faded, and the screen on the stage-curtains returned to just bright white. Then the machine switched itself off, the beam was extinguished, and the coloured spotlights resumed their eerie illumination of the hall.

Immediately, the trained parrots in the corner repeated their instructions, almost in the same tones as the children had just heard.

"Presssss the red button!"

"Presssss the green!"

Maxwell and Roberta stirred from their shell-shocked and dazed state, and gazed at the two cages.

"*No way, Pedro*!!" burst Roberta. "We're not sitting through that again! Come on, Ozzie, we've got to dismantle this lot, pronto! And we've still got to check on the squibbitz in the school-house...and *get back home*! If m'mum's taken me a bedtime glass of milk, I'm definitely for the high-jump!"

"Oh, don't worry! They'll still be tryin' to dance around the boxes of car-boot junk in the front room!" laughed Maxwell. "Nobody knows we've gone! That's for sure!"

But, as you know, Maxwell couldn't have been *more* wrong!!

Back at Chestnut Terrace, Mr Underdown was still pacing up and down the hedges that surrounded the field behind the house. He was about to try searching the graveyard.

Inside No.34, Mrs Nudd had calmed down a little, with the help of a couple of her tablets and a cup of sweet tea. All sorts of thoughts were still dashing through her mind but she kept telling herself that everything would turn out alright in the end. Everytime she heard a noise she pictured Roberta and Maxwell coming through the front door!

At about half-past eleven, the door-bell rang.

Mrs Nudd jumped off the settee and dashed down the hall.

Could it be? Could it be them?

She opened the door...and there, in the moonlight, stood a tall, burly, dark-haired policeman and a rather more chunky, blonde-haired police-woman.

"Good evenin', madam!" said the policeman. "Mrs Rita Nudd? No.34, Chestnut Terrace?"

Mrs Nudd nodded and invited them in. They stepped over all the boxes of junk, and Rita cleared a space for them on the settee in the front room.

She explained what had happened and after lots of embarrassing questions about whether mother and daughter and father and son had had any serious arguments and disagreements recently, they stood up, took the photos that Rita had provided and put away their notebooks.

"In ninety-nine cases out of a hundred, the kids come back within an hour or two!" said PC Clegg. "You've had no tiffs. You say they've taken no money or packed bags of food and clothes! They'll be back in no time, mark my words! They probably just decided to have a sneaky midnight feast somewhere! You know what youngsters are like!"

Rita nodded politely, but still had doubts in her mind.

"Let us know when they turn up!" reassured WPC Hopkins. "Meanwhile, we'll scout the streets in the squad car, and put a general alert out!"

With that, the police left and Mrs Nudd put the kettle on. She made herself a cup of tea and returned to the front room. It wasn't long before the front door-bell rang again.

She jumped up as though she'd been stung, spilled the tea all over the settee and the pile of old records, and dashed to the door.

This just *had* to be them!

It just *had* to be!

She pulled open the door...and there, to her great disappointment, was none other than *Lenny Underdown*, flanked by two *even more* burly policemen, each gripping one of his arms!

"Mrs Rita Nudd? No.34, Chestnut Terrace?" asked the taller one.

Rita nodded.

"Can you vouch for this man?" asked the other policeman. "We've just caught him sneaking around in the graveyard with a torch. Up to no good if you ask me! He says you'll identify him!"

Rita looked skywards and shook her head in disbelief.

She didn't know whether to laugh or cry!

"Just wait till I get my hands on that daughter of mine!!"

"And just wait till I get *my hands* on that *son* of mine!!" grumbled Mr Underdown as he wriggled free from the vice-like grip of the two policemen.

"Just wait!" they chorused.

"Just wait a minute!" hissed Grimmage, as he hobbled towards the great front door of Murkbog Towers. "Hold your horses!"
Once more, a loud volley of knocking almost shook the walls of the old, crumbling tower.
Grimmage unlocked the door, and in burst the larger than life figure of Titus Gutbucket, propelled by the howling, gushing wind behind him. Dressed in a long, blue raincoat and tall, matching headgear, almost like one of those old-fashioned top hats, he flew into the room. With his coat tails flapping like wings, his hat instantly took off and did a lap around the candelabra and landed smartly on the table like a small aeroplane.
The wind snatched at everything, blowing paper, cardboard, clothes and bedding sheets everywhere. The twelve candles just about clung on to their flames as they danced even more wildly, bending this way and that in unison, like a dozen line-dancers.
Grimmage struggled to close the door, but with the help of Mrs Grubbage and Mr Gutbucket, they finally managed to lock out the raging gale.
"What a dashed bad night this is, my man!" Titus exclaimed at last, stripping off his soggy raincoat to reveal his trade-mark pink suit with red and yellow spotted handkerchief sticking out of the breast pocket. "Still, if we play our cards right, the first part of our plan has been put into operation earlier this evening. It all went like clockwork! By the way, have you got any little treats for me to get m'choppers round? I'm starving!"
Grimmage and Grubbage looked at one another sheepishly, and silently shook their heads.
"We thought *you* might bring a spot of grub!" ventured Grimmage, a trifle nervously.

"Look, you dashed little worm!" growled Titus Gutbucket. "It's *me* doing all the hard work round here! It's *me* who's taking the risks! It's *me* who was humiliated in front of the whole world's television viewers just before Christmas! And it's *me* who lost millions of pounds, especially to that dashed Miss Leonora Divine!"

Grimmage offered him the last of his dry cream-crackers.

"And all you can offer is...*that*?" Titus glared, his black handle-bar moustache twitching with anger.

"I taught the parrots!" risked Grimmage, determined to point out his importance in the brewing plot. "Talking of which...what's *that* stuck to your foot, Mr Gutbucket?"

T.G. looked down to his mud splattered white shoes, and noticed two brightly coloured parrot feathers stuck to his soles.

"It's those two pesky parrots I left in the school-hall!" he said, nibbling on his cream-cracker. "They both got a bit uppity in their cages. Strange surroundings, I s'pose. They were flappin' 'n squawkin' like nobody's business, when I was trying to rig up all the electrics. Feathers were flying like crazy! Then they started pooing

all over the place! Never seen anything like it! Projectile poo squirting everywhere! Right through the cage bars! It was absolutely dis-gusting! What did you feed 'em on, man?"

Grimmage looked up at the tall, black haired Gutbucket, and a smile cracked across his reptilian mouth.

"Cream-crackersss!" he exploded, hardly being able to control a sudden and very rare burst of cackling laughter.

Titus Gutbucket, at once, in absolute disgust, spat out every morsel of what was in his mouth and threw the remains of his dry cracker into the fire.

"Trying to poison me, eh?" he growled, with a wild and wicked look in his eye. "I'll tell you this, my man. If *I* snuff it...if *I* bite the dust...then you two worms can definitely say goodbye to *ever* making a dashed fortune out of those little dashed creatures of yours!

Without my brains, you've well and truly *had it*!"

"Did everything go to plan, then?" asked Grubbage meekly, poking the fire into action viciously, as though she was poking Gutbucket.

"Of course, madam! Of course!" bragged T.G., gazing into the flames and sparks. "Come Monday morning, all at Chestnut School will know that we mean business! The message is ready for them to see and hear! A real video nasty! And what's more, I've also located that worm, Maxwell Underpants and his little girlfriend, Robbie Nudd! They've got a caravan behind Chestnut Terrace. Yes, my dears, 'Phase One' is almost complete...and 'Phase Two' is about to be put into operation!"

Chapter 7

As Grimmage, Grubbage and Gutbucket gazed blissfully into the flames of the fire at Murkbog Towers, at precisely two minutes past midnight, their brilliant 'Phase One' had just about been utterly and completely sabotaged by Maxwell and Roberta!
"Just the two parrots to get into the school-house, and check that all's OK in there!" said Roberta, dusting down her jumper and jeans.
"Cor! Have you seen the time?" exclaimed Maxwell, looking up at the hall clock. "It's gone midnight!"
"Just keep your fingers crossed that we haven't been missed!" said Roberta, scrambling up onto the stage.

They both looked around the hall in the moonlight. It looked a bit eerie, but at least it was all back to normal...how it had been left on Friday night. All the electronic wizardry had been unplugged, dismantled and hidden under the stage with all the props for nativity plays and the like. Maxwell had even risked life and limb climbing the caretaker's longest ladders to take down the revolving discs of colours which had been fixed to the spotlights. Robbie had cleared up the mess on the floor around the parrot cages, and drawn back the stage-curtains.
"I reckon that whoever set all that lot up was the same person who was hanging around the caravan!" suggested Maxwell with a smile,

feeling like a detective. "He must have stood in the parrot poo near the cages and got a feather stuck to his shoe!"

"The question is...*who was it*?" wondered Roberta. "And *how* did he get into the school?"

Maxwell fished in his pocket for the new key to the door at the back of the stage.

"I hope you guys are going to be OK in here," he said to the parrots in their cages. "There's plenty of company for you! Ten other parrots in fact!"

"Presssss the red button!" said one in that familiar, chilling voice.

"Presssss the green!" joined in the other, as the door swung open.

Suddenly, Roberta called from the centre of the stage...from the very spot where Grimmage's desk had stood for years and years, concealing the trap door that led to the secret passage under the school floorboards.

"Ozzie, look at this! Another feather! Stuck to the stage with parrot poo!" She examined the floor carefully.

"And look, there's a footprint next to the trap door...and another...and another!"

"Well, that's one question answered!" said Maxwell. "Now we know how *whoever-it-was* got in and out! The underground passage from the graveyard!"

"We're going to have to do something about that!" said Roberta. "It means that the enemy can come in and out whenever they want! Then they've only got to get through that door at the back of the stage to reach the squibbitz!"

"But we've blocked up the secret door in the angel gravestone!" Maxwell pointed out. "So how are they getting into the passage?" Roberta looked at Maxwell.

"It can only mean one thing!" she said in a low voice, as though hidden ears were behind the stage-curtains. "There must be *another* entrance!"

"And the only person who knows where that is...is *Grimbag*!!"

Quickly, Roberta brushed away the evidence with the stage broom hidden behind the curtains. "If only this was magic!" she imagined, pretending to ride it like a witch. "It could whisk us off into the night and take us straight to the enemy's lair!"

"Come on, Robbie!" insisted Maxwell, thinking of the time. "We'll need more than magic broomsticks to help us, if Rita and m'dad have noticed that we're not where we're supposed to be!"

Fortunately, all was well in the school-house. The branches of the huge, old chestnut tree were crammed with sleeping squibbitz and roosting parrots. Knowing that they'd be back on Sunday to feed and exercise them, they quickly released the two new parrots from their cages and closed and locked the door behind them.

A couple of minutes later, Roberta had hidden the classroom key behind the plantpot, and they were making their way hand-in-hand across the dark school playground.

Suddenly, a beam of light lit them up like night had turned to day! They squinted, and raised their arms to shield their eyes.

"Hold it right there!" a gruff voice barked out of the blackness.

Thoughts galloped through the children's minds.

Who could it be?

At nearly half-past midnight?

Could it be the school intruder?

Had he been waiting for them?

Meanwhile, at No.34, Lenny and Rita sat huddled together on the settee in the front room amid the mountains of junk.

"Half-past twelve!" grumbled Rita. "It's car-boot day in a few hours! I'll never be able to keep m'eyes open!"

"And we've still got to pack the Morris!" mumbled Lenny.

At that moment the doorbell rang, making them both jump off the settee like a couple of jack-in-the-boxes!

"It's them! It's them!" exclaimed Rita. "It must be!"

She darted down the hall followed by Lenny.

She swung the door open and there...standing all meek and mild with their heads bowed and their eyes guiltily staring at the doorstep, were Maxwell and Roberta. Behind them were PC Clegg and WPC Hopkins.

In a split second all Rita's anger and worry dissolved and she burst into floods of tears, throwing out open arms and giving the children the biggest bear hugs you could imagine!

They both felt the breath being squeezed out of their lungs and their faces becoming redder and redder. Whether that was due to embarrassment or sheer blood pressure it was hard to tell!

"Where *have* you two been?" Mrs Nudd blubbered. "We've been sat on the settee all night waiting for you!"

"I told you they'd turn up!" PC Clegg smiled.

"All's well that ends well!" grinned WPC Hopkins.

"And thank *you* very much!" said Mr Underdown.

"A good night's sleep and everything'll seem better tomorrow...I mean today!" laughed PC Clegg, looking at his watch. "So we'll be on our way!"

"Where did you find 'em?" asked Mr Underdown.

"At Chestnut Hill, would you believe?" the police lady replied. "You'd think they would have had enough of school by Friday afternoon, wouldn't you?"

"But there they were, bold as brass, holding hands, walking across the school yard!" added the policeman. "A right couple of love-birds!"

Now, as if their faces weren't red enough already, Maxwell and Roberta suddenly blushed almost crimson, wishing they could disappear into thin air, away from these terrible adults.

Roberta bit her lip, struggled out of the bear hug, pushed past Lenny and was just about to rush up the stairs to the sanctuary of her bedroom.

"You just stop there, madam!" shouted her mother from the front door. "Haven't you something to say to these kind, young constables?"

Roberta stopped on the bottom step and gathered herself.

"Thank you!" she said in her poshest, politest voice (the one she reserved for speaking to Mr Underdown).

Lenny nudged Maxwell.

"Thank you!" his son spluttered, stepping into the hall.

"And thank you from us two as well!" said Mr Underdown, beginning to close the door. "You've taken a great weight off our shoulders! Goodnight!"

"Just doin' our job, sir!" said PC Clegg. "Just wish more parents would do theirs! Good evening, sir...and madam!"

And with that final embarrassing little lesson from the policeman, the front door closed...and the two, now seething adults glared at their offspring.

I'll spare you the details of what followed next at No.34!

All I *will* say is that Rita's anger certainly returned!

Words such as '*grounded*!', '*that green stuff is coming straight out of your hair!*' and '*that's the end of the caravan for you, mate*!' bounced from wall to wall and rattled the vases on the stairs for the next twenty minutes.

When, at last the parental cannons ceased fire, Roberta sulked off up to her bedroom and Maxwell was given a sleeping-bag to curl up in behind the settee.

As they both tossed and turned trying to get to sleep, their minds buzzed with the events of the night and the battles that lay ahead...not only with the enemy...but now, on the home-front as well!!!

Chapter 8

Early on the Sunday morning, sunlight beamed into the front room and stirred Maxwell from his sleep behind the settee.

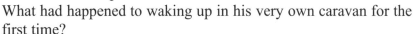

He rubbed his eyes and wondered where he was for a minute or two!

It was as though he'd shrunk to the size of an *Action Man* and woken up in a flower-bed in a public park! Roses, tulips, chrysanthemums and carnations were everywhere, and their scent, as usual, was almost over-powering!

With the floral wallpaper soaring above him on one side and the settee cover on the other...not to mention the flowers in the carpet pattern and the matching curtains...his bleary eyes were just about filled with petals!

What had happened to waking up in his very own caravan for the first time?

Then he remembered the events of the night before!

And his heart sank!

Looking like a giant yellow caterpillar, he rolled over in his sleeping-bag, sighed with dismay and eyed a larger than life spotted ladybird that adorned the wallpaper.

It was then that he realised just how quiet it was.

Not just the absence of buzzing bees and chirping crickets from his morning garden...but the absence of *everything*!

He forced his ears to listen as intensely as they could.

But there wasn't a single sound.

He stuck his fingers in his ears and wiggled them.

Had he been struck stone-deaf during the night?

He listened again.

And then he heard the ticking of clocks...several clocks...scattered all over the furniture in the front room.

He sat up and looked at them, one after the other.

Big clocks, small clocks, carriage clocks, alarm clocks, cuckoo clocks!

And all showing different times!

Suddenly, the cuckoo in the cuckoo clock shot out, and cuckooed!

Cuckoo! Cuckoo! Cuckoo! Cuckoo! Cuckoo! Cuckoo! Cuckoo!

Then, at the very same time as it sprung back into its clock, the front room door slowly opened and in walked Roberta, still with green, spiky hair. She was carrying a tray loaded with a strawberry milkshake, a thick piece of toast smothered in butter and a boiled egg in a pink egg-cup shaped like a duck!

"Rise and shine, Ozzie, my man! It's seven o'clock!" she giggled. "Sorry about the egg-cup! Hope you like your eggs well runny! Use the toast to mop it up!"

Maxwell gazed at his hostess in amazement!

Was this girl *never* down in the dumps?

"The place is empty!" she went on, with a wide grin. "The big 'uns departed about an hour ago to the car-boot, and best of all, they won't be back 'til late this afternoon! So we've got *all day* to get on with our little plans!"

"But, what about...?" wondered Maxwell.

"What about what, Sir Edward Maxwell Underdown?" laughed Roberta.

"I thought you were a famous, fearless intrepid explorer! Eat your boiled egg, drink your milk and let's get crackin'!"

"But what about being *'grounded'* and *'that's the end of the caravan and the green hair-do'*?"

"Look, Sir Edward," said Roberta, setting the tray down on the settee, "if we kids took notice of the big 'uns *all* of the time, there'd be *no* progress at all! We'd still be being shoved up chimneys, down coalmines, into cotton-mills and all the rest, where little 'uns are required! Sometimes you've just *got* to rebel and say 'no' for the sake of progress...and the generations of kids in the future! Right?"

"Right!" said Maxwell, crunching into his toast, and helpless to resist.

"So, we carry on as planned! OK?" urged Robbie.

"OK!"

Maxwell finished his breakfast and then helped with the washing-up and tidied the kitchen.

"Better get a few brownie-points under m'belt, in case the *big 'uns* suddenly appear out of the blue to check up on us!" suggested Maxwell, a bit anxiously.

"You're right, Ozzie!" grinned Roberta. "And whilst we're at it, let's vacuum all through, clean the windows, weed the back-garden, and have a cordon-bleu feast in the oven for when they get back!"

"You're jok...!" sighed Maxwell, swishing the soap suds down the plug-hole.

"Of course I am, you twit!" laughed Roberta. "Come on! Action stations!"

The rest of the day was brilliant! The Spring sun shone almost non-stop, and the two of them spent nearly all the time in the field giving the caravan its make-over. In next to no time they'd painted the outside in two tones of green...a dark green bottom

half and a light green top half. They even managed to paint the roof with the help of Rita's step-ladders. The dreadful pink gradually disappeared and by mid-morning the caravan was beautifully camouflaged and didn't stand out like a sore thumb anymore. Then they began to carry over from the house all the

gear they'd collected during the last few weeks. There were boxes of plastic greenery from all over Kirkthwaite! They'd called at all the charity shops, and asked supermarkets, food shops and florists if they'd hang on to any display material they were throwing out...as long as it was green! They'd even asked at the local rubbish tip! The result was a whole load of stuff that would transform the inside of the

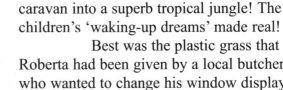

caravan into a superb tropical jungle! The children's 'waking-up dreams' made real!

Best was the plastic grass that Roberta had been given by a local butcher who wanted to change his window display. Two great, wide rolls of thick, soft grass which would completely carpet the caravan floor and make it all comfy and snug to walk on! Then there were all the artificial climbing plants they'd been given from a florist, and the thick and thin lengths of real bamboo from a furniture store. There were plastic pot plants with huge leaves, artificial

coconuts, palm tree branches, toy monkeys and parrots, not to mention a very realistic two metre long python! Maxwell had even found an unwanted sound-effect machine in a pet-shop! Luckily it was powered by batteries, and every time a button was pressed, different sounds of the jungle would play, from chattering monkeys and parrots, to waterfalls and buzzing insects, to pouring rain and gorillas grunting and beating their chests!

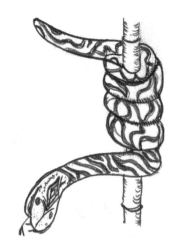

By two o'clock in the afternoon the caravan's make-over was just about complete...and it looked fantastic!

Stepping into it now was like setting foot in *Tarzan's* tree house in the middle of a jungle, or a castaway's hut on a tropical island! When Maxwell and Roberta finally stopped, sat down at the table and ate some fruit and cake from No.34, they looked around at what they'd created with a mixture of pride and wonder. It really *did* feel that they were in the middle of a South American rain forest,

instead of in a field on the edge of Kirkthwaite in Yorkshire, England!

"Can you hear the waters of the Amazon flowing by?" whispered Maxwell, cupping his hand to his ear and glancing at the bamboo roller blind he'd fixed to the window.

"Yes, and I can hear canoes being paddled upstream!" whispered Roberta, patting the skin of a tom-tom drum with the palms of her hands. "I just hope the locals are friendly! Perhaps we ought to send them a message on this!"

"Or we'll have a fire outside one day and send smoke signals!" beamed Maxwell, lost in his new world.

"Now before we get carried away, Ozzie," said Roberta, "we've still *another* job to do before we get back to the house and turn on the charm!"

"Of course, the squibbitz!" gasped Maxwell. "We've still got to feed and exercise them! Come on, let's get going! I just hope they're OK, and Grimmage hasn't been up to his tricks again!"

With a quick burst of chattering monkeys and parrots filling the caravan, Maxwell closed the door and followed Robbie across the field. Little did they know that hidden behind a clump of yellow gorse bushes in the far corner was a crouching figure....a crouching figure with a twitching black, handle-bar moustache, a spotted bow-tie and white shoes...spying on the two-tone green caravan with a pair of binoculars.

'So they reckoned *that* would work, did they?' he thought, with an evil look in his eyes. 'Paint it green and it would dashed well disappear, eh?'

He smiled to himself and stroked his moustache.

'I'll show those little worms who can make little caravans disappear...*for good*!!'

Ten minutes later, Maxwell and Roberta were just about to open the door at the back of the stage that led to the school-house.

"Keep your fingers crossed!" whispered Roberta, as she pushed open the door.

Fortunately, everything was fine, just as it had been the night before. They crunched through the brown and yellow horse chestnut leaves and were immediately surrounded by the wonderful squibbitz. Sunlight was pouring through the windows, illuminating all the fabulous creatures as they hopped around, nibbling nuts, plastic cups, newpaper and pieces of wood with their long, sharp front teeth.

Their colours ranged from dark grey to dark brown, and they were mostly about the size of rabbits, but with the bushy tails of squirrels curled over their arched backs. Long, furry ears flopped down over their faces, although they could make them stand straight up if they became alarmed or inquisitive. Their smaller front paws had three stubby fingers and a thumb for gripping food and climbing, each with a sharp, long claw. Hind feet were huge in comparison...long and flat like a hare's or a small kangaroo's, each foot having four little toes with shorter claws. Eyes  were generally dark brown but always enormous and above a pink twitching nose with plenty of long, silver, quivering whiskers. They were true omnivores...eaters of *everything*!!

From chalk to ink, from cardboard to leather, from autumn leaves to bicycle tyres, from milk cartons to plastic rulers, from washing-up liquid to paint brushes.

Literally *anything*!

So, not only did they look cute but with their fondness for rubbish, they were pretty useful, too!

It was no wonder at all that Grimmage, Grubbage and Gutbucket thought they were on to a winner before Christmas! Breeding them and selling them to the world at ridiculously high prices!

But it was one additional little talent that made the squibbitz *really* hot property!

The fact that they could *talk*!

Now, *that* was something special!

The only talking mammals on the planet other than humans!

With the help of the parrots, which were all now perched up in the branches of the tree, preening themselves, Grimmage had taught them quite a few words strung together into phrases.

Phrases such as:

"Good morning! Did you sleep well?"
"Hello and how are you? I'm very well, thankyou!"
"Can I have some food? I'm starving!"
"Let me out of my cage! I'm bursting!"
"What are *you* looking at? It's rude to stare!"
and, of course...
"I'll have your gutsss for gartersss!"

Maxwell and Roberta had managed amazingly to keep the creatures a total secret from the rest of the world for the last three months. The only other person to have set eyes on them (besides Grimmage and Grubbage) was Miss Teezil...and she had been sworn to secrecy.

They'd exercised them down the underground passage to the graveyard and even at night in the school-hall. Food was always fairly easy to find for them, but the sheer *amount* was sometimes a problem, as you can imagine! A hundred bottom-less pits take some filling!

So, amid the usual chaos when the children arrived, Maxwell climbed down to the old cages under the hall where they stored the bags and sacks of food, and Roberta started pumping water into buckets and troughs from the water-pump at the foot of the horse chestnut tree.

Soon, the squibbitz were tucking in to piles of wood shavings, sawdust and assorted off-cuts from the local saw-mill and lapping up the freshly drawn water...and the ten parrots, plus the two new ones, were ravenously eating their seeds and peanuts.

"I'm afraid we haven't got time to exercise you all today!" whispered Roberta, as she tickled a squibbit under the chin.

Maxwell's favourite squibbit, Zziffo (the one that had nibbled a hole in one of his dad's precious dancing shoes) was perched on his shoulder like a tame squirrel.

"Me Zziffo! How are you?" squeaked the squibbit.

"Very well, thankyou!" replied Maxwell, handing Zziffo a small slice of chipboard.

"Good boy, Zziffo! Me good boy?" the cute ball of fur chirped.

But before Maxwell could reply, Zziffo dropped the piece of wood, his eyes opened even wider than usual and his floppy ears suddenly stood straight up in the air.

He'd spotted something behind Maxwell that scared him.

Maxwell slowly turned, dreading what he'd see!

The door to the stage, inch by inch, was creaking open...

...and then...there...

      ...was a sight...

            ...that would chill *anyone* to the bone...!!

Chapter 9

A moment later, with a wild flurry of bushy tails, sawdust, splashing water and autumn leaves, every single squibbit had shot up into the safe branches of the chestnut tree!

There they sat in complete silence, ears all erect, gazing, horror-struck, at the fearsome sight below.

Maxwell put an arm around Roberta as they, too, stared at who had just come through the door. They nervously shuffled backwards amongst the crunching leaves, as though trying to escape from the creature's monstrous stare.

Neither the children nor the squibbitz had seen him in the flesh since before Christmas. The giant head projected onto the stage-curtains the night before had been horrific enough...but here...was the real thing!!

"So, we meet again, you evil little wormsss!" Grimmage spluttered from his brown, tobacco stained lips as he stepped further into his old home.

"I wishhh I could sssay that it wasss a pleasure to be back!" he hissed, glaring around the walls of the school-house and up into the chestnut tree, scaring the squibbitz even more.

He was dressed in an old, tatty, creased dark suit and waistcoat with great, mud splattered, black boots on his feet. There was quite a gap between the bottom of his trousers and his boots, revealing his scrawny legs and ankles covered in bright yellow socks with holes in them. He looked grubby, unshaven and unwashed. In fact he looked as though he'd been sleeping rough, on the streets, for months! Maxwell and Roberta just stared at the sight before them, speechless. "I sssee you've been looking after my preciousss friendsss!" he wheezed, looking into the branches. "Not for very much longer though, my little wormsss, not for very much longer!! Lisssten, and lisssten well!

Every sssingle one of them will be back in my possssessssion by the end of the week! You mark my wordsss!!"

His hideous, reptile face then took on a look of anger...one the children had seen before, when he was the headmonster of Chestnut Hill.

"And what have you done with the sssplendid work of my friend, Missster Titusss Gutbucket?" he growled.

He suddenly raised the volume of his voice.

"I have come to inssspect hisss effortsss...and all hasss been dessstroyed...

...*BY YOU TWO WORMSSS*!!"

Maxwell and Roberta stepped back a couple more paces, wondering what was coming next!

Suddenly, he produced from behind his back an ancient mobile phone, almost the size of a house brick!

He waved it in the air at the children.

Then came his next deadly announcement.

His voice dropped to a quiet hiss.

"If you two think you've defeated usss, got one up on usss...then think again! You may have ruined the firssst part of our plan...!"

He stepped forward and again waved the house brick at Maxwell and Roberta.

"...but *I* will *alwaysss* have the lassst laugh...and sssweet *revenge*! My friend, Titusss, has just informed me that he hasss jussst taken something very, very preciousss to *you*!! Sssweet, sssweet revenge!!"

With that, he laughed, turned and vanished through the door as quickly as the children had ever seen him move! The door closed with a bang.

"After him!" shouted Roberta.

A moment later they were both standing on the stage staring down at the trap door. Grimmage had gone.

"If only we could follow him and find out where the other entrance is!" sighed Roberta.

"Don't worry, we *will*!" insisted Maxwell, locking the stage-door. "But not now! We've *got* to get back home, before dad and Rita return from the car-boot! Come on, let's leg it!"

Fifteen minutes later, in the hall at No.34, Roberta's charm offensive was in full swing...or, rather, *almost* in full swing! Maxwell was proving to be a reluctant pupil.

"Look," said Robbie, "when they walk in the door, if the first thing they see...is us two dancing the tango...believe me, their little hearts will dissolve like sugar in cups of tea...and all that business last night will be forgotten! Trust me! OK?"

Maxwell wasn't at all convinced and it seemed a lot of messing around, doing all this drippy dancing...and then it might not work after all!

"You mean all their angry threats about your green hair, and us being grounded and me losing the caravan, will just vanish! Just like that?" he mumbled, as the Latin American music filled the house.

"It's an absolute certainty!" laughed Robbie. "They won't be able to

resist *oohing* and *ahhing* as soon as they come through the front door! '*Ah, bless 'em!*' m'mum'll drool...and '*he takes after me, you know!*' your dad'll boast! They'll be as pleased as Punch to see us dancing!"

Maxwell had been shown a few steps by Rita and Lenny in the last few months, but never by Roberta!

As she grabbed hold of him and started ordering his big feet around, he felt himself blushing redder and redder!

"Right, now this next bit's very dramatic!" she enthused, taking a plastic rose from a vase on the stairs and clenching it between her jaws.

"Now, I'll lean backwards!" she spluttered, while trying to grip the rose in her mouth, "and you lean over me, look really grim and serious and twist your head to one side. Remember, you're supposed to be a matador...a bullfighter...and I'm supposed to be a bull you fancy...or something like that!"

Maxwell could hardly believe what he was doing. He felt ridiculous, especially being so much taller than Robbie!

"You're absolutely *sure* about this?" he grumbled, as the exciting rhythm seemed to carry them down the hall towards the front door. Louder and louder the music swelled...

And then, suddenly...the door burst open and in fell Rita and Lenny, each with a box of junk from the car-boot.

They stopped dead in their tracks and gazed open-mouthed over the tops of the boxes at their two offspring.

"Well, well, well! Just look at that, Lenny!" exclaimed Mrs Nudd, with a tear coming to her eye. "Ah, bless 'em!"

"Well, I never thought I'd see the day!" beamed Mr Underdown. "He takes after me, you know!"

Maxwell winked at Roberta and, believe it or not, not a single word was said all Sunday evening about the little adventure on Saturday night. Not a single word. The charm offensive had worked a treat, helped, of course, by the fact that Rita and Lenny had brought back lots of fantastic new junk from the car-boot to chat about and examine.

As usual, they'd sold about *three* boxes of rubbish...but returned with *four* boxes...so the mountains of junk in every room became that little bit higher.

After a delicious late tea of Lenny's famous '*spag-bol*', as he called it, Maxwell began to wonder whether he'd be able to have his first night in the caravan.

"Fantastic spaghetti bolognese, dad!" he burst, licking his lips and quickly perfecting Robbie's '*charm technique*'!

"Thanks, son!" replied Mr Underdown, with a smile. "It's the sauce that does it, you know! Not only *deee-licious*, but very *nutricious*! It'll put hairs on your chest!"
"I hope it doesn't put hairs on *my* chest!" giggled Robbie in her best 'good-as-gold', 'butter-wouldn't-melt-in-her-mouth' voice.
"No, my little princess," Lenny reassured her. "There'll be no chance of that, pet!"
"Now, after you and Maxwell have washed up," he went on, trying to change the subject, "I think me and Rita'll show you both a few more tango steps!"
Maxwell and Roberta glanced at one another, both knowing exactly what the other was thinking!
'*Oh No*!! *But worth it under the present circumstances*!
Grin and bear it...stiff upper lip and all that!'
"We would *love* to!" grinned Roberta, pinching Maxwell's knees under the table, until he winced.
"Yeah! That'll be well good! Brill!" screamed Maxwell under torture.
"What a *wonderful* way to spend a Sunday evening!"

By the time the cuckoo clock let them all know it was eight o'clock, Maxwell reckoned he'd suffered enough and thought it worth asking about sleeping in the caravan.
"Dad..." he began, keeping his fingers tightly crossed.
"What's up, son?" said Mr Underdown, polishing one of his prized records on his sleeve. "Do you want to know more about the amazing tango? You know they used to call me *Romeo Tango* when me and your mother used to dance all over Engla...."
"Yes, dad, I know. You've told me a thousand times!
No, what I was wondering is...tonight, whether I can slee...!"
Suddenly, a scream came from the top of the stairs, so shrill and loud that Lenny dropped the record, and Mrs Nudd nearly spilled another cup of tea!
It was Roberta.
"Whatever's the matter, darling?" called Rita.

"Come up here! All of you!" shouted Robbie.

Lenny, Rita and Maxwell pelted up the stairs, knocking vases of flowers flying, wondering what on earth all the fuss was about...what possible emergency there could be! They were immediately ushered into Roberta's bedroom.

"Look through the window!" exclaimed Robbie, almost panic stricken, and as angry and flustered as Maxwell had ever seen her. "Look in the field! Ozzie's caravan's *gone*! *Vanished into thin air*!"

Chapter 10

"So, Mr Underdown," concluded PC Clegg, at around half-past-ten on the Monday morning, "you're telling me that you are *now* missing a small caravan...and let me get this right...the colour of the said vehicle is bright pink with a spot of green!"
Lenny nodded, as the constable scribbled in his note-book.
"You've had quite a weekend in one way or another!" remarked WPC Hopkins. "What with the kids going missing, then you being picked up in the graveyard...and now the caravan going walkabout!"
Lenny nodded again. He scratched his head and sipped his mug of tea. He was feeling a little dozy, not having quite woken up yet. In fact, he'd only just crawled out of bed. Rita had gone to work after breakfast and Maxwell and Roberta had gone to school.
"Well at least it should be easy to spot, being *that* colour!" laughed PC Clegg. "You don't see pink caravans everyday!"
Lenny smiled a dozy smile and secretly wished the constables would leave him to his usual Monday morning peace and quiet.
"And, of course, we *do* have two splendid clues as to the vehicle that towed the missing vehicle off the field!" said the police-lady.
"What's that then?" said Lenny, suddenly perking up.
"We've spotted tyre marks across the field!" explained WPC Hopkins.
"Some sort of gigantic, gas-guzzling four-b'-four, by the look of 'em!

And, then there's *this*!"
From behind her back she produced a
huge, smashed wing-mirror.
"Wow!" gasped Lenny, waking up
even more. "Where did *that* come
from?"
"By one of the gate-posts! The thief's

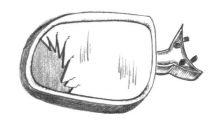

vehicle must have had a real squeeze to get through! It was simply
ripped off!"
Then she turned the wing-mirror over.
Lenny gasped again.
It was *bright pink*!
"The thief must have wanted a pink caravan to go with his pink four-
b' -four!" continued PC Clegg. "He spotted it and pinched it, just like
that!"
"And there's only one guy in these parts who owns a monstrous
bright pink tank of a vehicle!" said WPC Hopkins, with a gleam in
her blue eyes.
"Who's that then?" burst Lenny.
"Ah, sir, we're not at liberty to disclose the name at this point in our
investigations!" said PC Clegg. "But we will be travelling from here
to his disgustingly enormous pink mansion to locate his disgustingly
enormous pink vehicle with its missing disgustingly enormous wing-
mirror!"
"I take it this wealthy geezer's not the flavour of the month down at
the local cop-shop!" Lenny smiled.
"Sorry, sir! Can't say any more now," said the beaming police-man,
"but we've been trying to pin something on this bloke for years! He's
a nasty, greedy piece of work! And *this* could just be what we've
been waiting for!"

    With that, the two police constables left No.34
and Mr Underdown thankfully lowered himself onto the settee in the
front room, found the television's remote-control and lazily pressed a
button. He was looking forward to a nice couple of hours of relaxing
morning telly...just to calm his nerves, he told himself, as he
continued to sip from his mug of tea. A bit of peace and quiet.

Meanwhile, at Chestnut Hill Juniors, the bell was just ringing for morning break. In Class 4, Maxwell and Roberta were standing anxiously by Miss Teezil's desk. They were keen to tell her about the events of the weekend, especially concerning the intruders into the school and the threats from Grimmage.

"So '*Revenge is Sweet*' is it?" said the small, plump Miss Teezil at last, with a determined look in her blue eyes under her mass of spiky black hair. "We'll see about that!"

She looked at Roberta's new hairstyle.

"Matches mine!" she said with a grin. "Do you think green will suit *me*?"

Roberta smiled.

"Yes, Miss, you'll look well good! And if *you* have it done, m'mum'll think it's OK for me to be green! She's not too keen at the moment!"

"Go on, Miss! Go for it!" urged Maxwell.

"Alright, alright, you two, we'll see...now back to more important matters! First, we've got to block the trap door on the stage. I'll get the caretaker and a couple of his mates to move the baby grand piano from the hall floor and make sure one of its legs is on top of the trap door! That should solve *that* little problem!"

Maxwell and Roberta nodded enthusiastically in agreement, both of them picturing an angry Grimmage trying to push his way up into the school, the next time he wanted to pay a secret visit!

"We've changed all the locks, and strengthened the windows in the schoolhouse, so the squibbitz should be secure!" Miss Teezil went on, like an army officer addressing her troops. "But we've got to be ready for whatever Grimmage, Grubbage and Gutbucket try on next!"

Suddenly, the sound of a peeping car-horn came from the front of the school. "Ah, that'll be our brand new pupils!" said Miss Teezil, in the blink of an eye

changing from sergeant-major to headmistress. "They're twins...your age! Their mother's decided to move them from some fancy, expensive school in the sticks to Chestnut Hill. Money problems I think...finding it difficult to pay the fees! Still, we'll give them a superb education here, won't we? Do you think you two could possibly look after them for me? Show them the ropes!"
Despite having a lot on their plates at the moment, Maxwell and Roberta were only too happy to assist the wonderful Miss Teezil. "Come on, then!" she bubbled. "Let's go and meet the little darlings!"

As the rather posh, chauffeur driven, raspberry coloured Ferrari sports car screeched off down the street, the twins...two girls...stood there looking up at their new school. They had looks of sheer disgust on their faces, as though they were staring at a wet, slimy slug crawling over a lettuce leaf in a salad. As an educational establishment it was *not quite* what they were used to!

Where were the tennis courts and the tree-lined drives? Where was the swimming-pool and the tranquil rose garden for peaceful meditation?
Chestnut Hill's front door opened and the small reception party stood on the top step.
"Smile, smile!" the twins suddenly whispered to one another out of the sides of their mouths. In a trice, their expressions changed and they became the delightful, well-mannered girls they had been told to be by their mother.
They were absolutely identical! Both with long, shining jet black hair, dark olive skin and brown eyes. Both were wearing identical yellow, flowery dresses, knee length white socks and white sandals. They looked as though they'd just flown in from Spain or Greece.
"Very Mediterranean!" beamed Miss Teezil, gliding down the steps, her arms outstretched in welcome.

"You are right, *senora*!" said the slightly taller twin.
"Our *madre*...our mother...is *Espanol*...Spanish...from the city of
Madrid! *Buenos dias, senora*! *Como esta*?"
(Good day, madam! How are you?)
Miss Teezil was very impressed by her two new
charges and shook their hands warmly. She could instantly see that
they could be useful in the classroom with language teaching and
learning about Spain.
"*Muy bien, gracias*! *Me llamo Miss Teezil*!" she ventured uncertainly
in her holiday Spanish.
(Very well, thankyou! My name is Miss Teezil)
The twins continued to smile politely and shook hands with Maxwell
and Roberta. Occasionally, as Robbie noticed, they kept looking at
one another and raising their eyes to the skies, as if wondering what
on earth they were doing there in the first place.
"Maxwell and Roberta will...look...after...you...while...you...settle...
in," said Miss Teezil, with great gaps between the words.
"There...is...a...desk...ready...for...you...in...the...classroom!"
"Miss Teezil, before we carry on," said the other twin rather firmly,
"we've got to tell you that we were *born* in England and we
understand *every single word*!"
The headmistress was slightly embarrassed.
"I apologise." she said softly. "I wasn't thinking. I hope you will
forgive me!"
The twins nodded and smiled sweetly, before once again rolling their
eyes to the heavens.
"By the way," carried on Miss Teezil, "your *madre*...sorry, your
mother, didn't tell me your names!"
Expecting them to be called something like Isabella and Elena, Ana
and Maria or Rosa and Dolores, she and Maxwell and Roberta had
quite a shock when they said, one after the other...the taller one first...
"My name is *Honeysuckle*!"
"And my name is *Daffodil*! Our mother just loves *flores*... flowers!"
Maxwell and Roberta looked at one another in amazement, the exact
same thought running through their minds,
'Just like someone else we know!'

By the end of the day Honeysuckle and Daffodil had settled into Class 4 very well. In fact *so well*, that for the last half-an-hour before home time, they managed to teach the whole class how to count from one to ten in Spanish!

At just before three-thirty, with Miss Teezil conducting from the her desk, the class chorused,

"*uno...*   (oo-no)
  dos...   (dohs)
    tres...   (trehs)
      cuatro... (kwah-tro)
        cinco... (theen-co)
          seis...   (sehs)
            siete... (see-eh-tay)
              ocho... (oh-cho)
                nueve... (nweh-veh)
                  diez..."   (dee-ez)

and then burst out into excited applause!

Miss Teezil smiled with delight, the children put their chairs on their desks and were sent home with a cheerful '*See you all tomorrow*!'

"Have you enjoyed your first day?" she asked the twins.

"We have!" replied Honeysuckle, "and we are looking forward to *manana*...tomorrow!"

"And have Maxwell and Roberta looked after you well?"

"They have!" replied Daffodil, with a strange gleam in her eye. "And they have kindly invited us to their house after school tomorrow. We can't wait!!"

Once again, they raised their eyes to the heavens...but then they winked at one another...as their little plot thickened!

Chapter 11

Early the following morning as the thick mists swirled around Murkbog Towers, an enormous pink four-by-four was bumping along the pot-holed track towards the crumbling ruins. Titus Gutbucket was at the wheel and was far from enjoying the ride. "Ghastly track!" he grumbled, as he tried to guide his tank between the water-filled holes, dreading that one might be a bottomless pit which would swallow him up and his gas-guzzler forever!
"Why haven't those two dashed worms fixed these holes yet?" he cursed.

The broken shape of the ruin slowly, and almost magically, formed before his eyes in the distance. It looked like something straight out of a horror movie! He imagined spooky bats circling around the jagged walls, fearful ghosts roaming the cellars with clanking chains, not to mention starving packs of howling, ravenous wolves stalking the moors.
He gazed around with his eyes staring wildly. He was letting his imagination get the better of him...and, at the same time, taking his eyes off the track!
Suddenly, without warning, the front of his tank lurched downwards, throwing Gutbucket hard against the steering wheel.
"Curse, curse and curse again!" he yelled.
The front wheels had plunged into a deep pot-hole.

Gutbucket opened his door, plunged his white shoes into the muddy water, and inspected the damage.

"Call yourself a four-b'-four, do you?" he shouted, as he slammed his hand on the pink bonnet. "Right, we'll see what you're made of!"

He climbed back inside, threw the gear-stick into reverse and pressed the accelerator with all the strength he could muster. The engine revved like a rocket taking off...and then the great, pink monstrosity shot backwards at the speed of light...and straight into another whopping water-filled pot-hole!

As he hammered the steering wheel with his clenched fists, Gutbucket cursed Grimmage and Grubbage even more!

And then, to make things even worse, the engine spluttered to a stop and the headlight beams were extinguished.

Gutbucket sat there...in the complete silence of the swirling, thick mist.

He squinted through the windscreen, but all he could see was mist, mist and more mist.

And it was then...that he heard the howling.

A strange, distant howling.

He shook his head and poked a finger in his hairy ear and wiggled it around.

Was he hearing things?

His imagination was beginning to get the better of him again.

He imagined the pack of marauding, skinny wolves searching for food!

They'd sniff his scent!

Close in for the kill!

Surround his gas-guzzler!

One would pounce...and that would be th...

Suddenly the strange howl cut through the silence again!

Closer this time!

And then again, and again.

A blood-curdling sound, the like of which he'd never heard in his life.

Then, all at once, from the rear, bright white light flooded the inside of his vehicle.

What was happening?

Was he going to be attacked?

Hit over the head...mugged...robbed...?

In a panic, his shaking hand switched on the ignition.

The huge engine exploded into life...and then spluttered out.

He tried again!

"Excuse me, sir, can we have a word?" came a small voice from behind.

This time the engine roared into life...and drowned out the voice. Gutbucket didn't hear it.

He threw the gear-stick into forward, pressed the accelerator and revved the engine as hard as he could. The great, rear wheels whined and spun wildly sending mud and water shooting backwards like a nasty, brown, horizontal waterfall from a bursting dam!

But, the monstrous gas-guzzler stayed exactly where it was...stuck fast!

He released the accelerator and turned the engine off angrily.

It was then that Gutbucket noticed that the bright white light from behind had gone.

He turned and looked through his rear window.

And there...standing perfectly still like two statues with their arms out sideways and completely covered from head to toe in dripping mud...were two figures! Men or women he couldn't tell!

One of them, the taller one, slowly moved its arm...and a brown, dripping hand wiped a brown, dripping face.

Then the figure walked stiffly and uncomfortably forward...followed by the shorter figure.

"Excuse me, sir," said PC Clegg, with a wicked smile on his mud streaked face. "Apologies about our wailing siren, by the way, sir. Hope it didn't alarm you! Needs fixing! Sounds like a wolf howling!"

He paused, and although he was drenched to the skin, he was enjoying the moment.

"We saw you on the main road and couldn't help noticing that you had a missing wing-mirror!"

A dripping WPC Hopkins, her blonde hair now chocolate brown, then rather stiffly, with squelchy footsteps, joined her colleague. She produced from behind her back the missing wing-mirror.

"We think *this* may be the little darling in question!" she said with a satisfied smile, as she placed it in position on the vehicle.

"Fits perfectly!" exclaimed PC Clegg, as though he was the prince in *Cinderella*.

"W...well, that's...that's v...very kind of you to re...return it, constables!" stuttered a very humble Mr Gutbucket. "You've g...gone to a lot of tr...trouble!"

"Talking of *trouble*, sir...I'm afraid it's *you* who's *in it*!" smiled the sodden, squelchy, but cheerful police-lady.

"In fact, *in it* up to your eye-balls, sir!" smirked PC Clegg.

"Why's that, constable?" said Gutbucket, as calmly and innocently as he could.

"You see, sir," whispered the drenched policeman, leaning forward and dripping all over Mr Gutbucket, "this 'ere wing-mirror is a piece of evidence in future *criminal proceedings*!!"

"How dashed *dare* you, young man?" snapped Gutbucket, at last beginning to revert to his normal self. "I hope you're not suggesting what I *think* you're dashed suggesting!"

"We dashed *are*, sir!" replied the determined policeman. "A little matter of stolen property involving this particular vehicle in the actual robbery!"

"But, but...," spluttered Gutbucket, reaching for a twenty pound note from his wallet. "Do you know who *I am*? And more to the point...do you know who *I know* in the highest ranks of the County's police force?"

"Firstly, we *do* know who you are...a certain Mr Titus 'Good-for-nothing' Gutbucket, swanning around in your great, monstrous, gas-guzzling, air polluting tin can!" said WPC Hopkins with a grin.

"And if you are trying to *bribe* us into saying *nothing* about this little robbery in which you were involved," said PC Clegg with a serious look on his mud-caked face, and reaching for his soaked note-book, "then *that* is yet *another* offence!"

He paused, licked the end of his pencil and looked at Gutbucket, like another slug on another lettuce leaf.

"So what have we got, so far?" he continued, scribbling on the soggy pages.

"Theft of a certain vehicle...driving without due care with a missing wing-mirror...assaulting Her Majesty's Constabulary with mud...and bribery! I think that should do very nicely, sir. We will look forward immensely to meeting you again in court! Good morning, sir!"

With that, the constables sploshed back to their patrol-car and reversed down the track into the thickening mist.

Titus Gutbucket sat all alone in his stranded tin can, fuming like a volcano about to erupt.

Slowly, he reached into his jacket pocket and grasped a white

envelope, with a typed address, beginning '*The Headmistress, Chestnut Hill Junior School*'...

He looked at it with evil eyes, and even though he was seething and steaming with anger, a devious and cunning smile cracked across his scheming face.

"Just wait until she reads *this*!" he croaked to himself venomously, "Just wait until she reads *this*!"

Chapter 12

Tuesday at school went like clockwork and everyone enjoyed the day. Miss Teezil again made use of her two new pupils...this time, to have a *Spanish Day*!
The chauffeur driven, raspberry sports car brought not only the twins but a whole load of Spanish gear for the pupils in Class 4 to examine. There were hats and dresses, books and magazines, maps and flags, Euro notes and coins, foods and drinks, ornaments, toys and games. In fact, by the time it was scattered all over the desks, the classroom looked like one of Rita and Lenny's car-boot sales!
During the morning the children wrote a story about a Spanish holiday that went wrong, learned a few more Spanish phrases, and chanted the five-times-table in Spanish. Lunch was a super *Paella*, made to perfection by the new cook, Mrs Pepper...and then, during the afternoon, geography, art and craft and drama definitely had a Mediterranean feel!

All through the day the twins were friendly and chatty to everyone, although Roberta noticed them occasionally whispering to one another behind cupped hands. And when she and Maxwell closed the stage-curtains after lunch so they could open the door into the school-house to feed the squibbitz...Roberta spotted them sneaking a crafty peek!

As everyone put their things away at the end of the day, Roberta whispered to Maxwell.

"There's something about those two that niggles me! They're up to mischief, I'm certain! But I can't put my finger on *what* it is!"

"Well I think they're OK!" whispered Maxwell. "And I think it was ace of you to invite them to No.34 for tea!"

"I did it to please Miss Teezil!" admitted Roberta. "I should have waited! I just don't trust them, the more I see them together. It's all that whispering in corners as though they're plotting something! And all that looking up to the heavens, as though they're too good for us common folk!"

"You mean they're evil, deceiving, scheming snobs, to put it in a nutshell!" smiled Maxwell, giving her a quick peck on the cheek. "I *do* like the way you always tell it how it is!!"

"Ozzie!" Robbie gasped, quickly blushing. "You can't do *that* in broad daylight, in the classroom! You'll have everyone talking!"

Maxwell sat down, lifted his desk lid and took out his homework. Suddenly, Daffodil crept up behind Roberta from nowhere.

"I see Maxwell likes you very, very much!" she giggled, looking at Roberta with her mischievous, brown eyes. "I'll let you into a little secret! My sister likes Maxwell, too. You'd better watch out! Honeysuckle's a lot taller than you, you little shrimp! So he won't have to bend as far to kiss her!"

Walking home to No.34 wasn't much fun for anyone! Maxwell and Roberta walked hand-in-hand, Roberta quietly fuming and hardly saying a word....while the twins skulked behind, carrying two large, traditional, red and black, Spanish dancing dresses, which Miss Teezil thought Rita and Lenny would like to see.

"What a quaint little house!" said Daffodil, once they reached the front door. "We, of course, live in a grand mansion with over *fifty* rooms!"

"Well I bet none are as beautifully decorated as the ones you are about to see!" said Maxwell, trying to support Roberta.

Robbie opened the door and the four children stepped into the hall. Immediately, the twins burst into fits of laughter.

"We thought *our* mother liked flowers...but *this*!" scoffed Honeysuckle, clicking her tongue and looking disgusted. "It's absolutely ridiculous! And look at all these boxes of rubbish!!"
Roberta saw red!
She'd just about had enough!
"Now, look you two!" she snapped. "We've had the good manners to invite you two *sisters-from-hell* for tea with my mum and Ozzie's dad! If you're going to be *pains in the backside* all evening then you can sling your hooks now and *clear off*! Got it?"
The sisters launched into a flood of Spanish at one another.
"OK, OK! We apologise!" said Honeysuckle, blinking her large, dark eyes meekly. "We will be on our best behaviour from now on! We shake your hands! OK?"
At the bottom of the stairs the four politely shook hands. Honeysuckle particularly enjoyed contact with Maxwell, and squeezed his hand extra tightly, much to his embarrassment. Then she gazed up into his freckles and fluttered her eyelids. Roberta noticed and glared at her rival with daggers almost flying out of her eyes!
It was certainly going to be an *uneasy* peace!

Tuesday night, as always, was *'fish 'n' chips night'*, and although the twins expressed words of enthusiasm, Roberta could tell that the English delicacy was going to go down like a lead balloon! Nevertheless she and Maxwell quickly nipped

down to the chippie so that it would all be ready for when Rita got in from work after picking Lenny up from the pub. They left the twins buttering sliced white bread and brewing a pot of tea.

When they returned with the warm, newspaper parcels, Honeysuckle and Daffodil gave them their usual disdainful look. A look of sheer haughtiness and scorn, mixed with contempt and tinged with utter superiority!

"You get your food wrapped in *newspaper*?" gasped Daffodil, unable to help herself.

"You think we are tramps? You insult us!" joined in Honeysuckle. "We are used to eating out of silver tureens, with silver knives and forks, and the very best china!"

At that moment, the cuckoo clock cuckooed six o'clock and...bang on time...Rita and Lenny burst through the front door, tossed their coats onto the coat hooks and immediately switched on the record-player in the hall! Seconds later, as the rhythms of Latin-America filled the house once again, the two crazy adults had plastic roses clenched between their teeth and were dancing the tango up and down the hall carpet, in between the boxes of junk.

From the kitchen, the two visitors stared in disbelief!

First, they'd come into a house the size of a shoe-box!

Second, they'd never seen as much tasteless decor...or, as much junk!

Third, they were going to have to eat out of newspapers...swallow sliced, white bread that looked and felt like soft polystyrene...and drink that horrid English drink named after a letter of the alphabet!

And now, to top it all, the quaint little house had turned into a mad dance-hall with a couple of maniacs strutting about like a pair of demented peacocks!!

They could hardly stand it any longer!

Should they make a run for it?

They looked at one another!

But it was too late!

One of the demented peacocks suddenly noticed the Spanish dresses lying across the settee in the front room.

Mrs Nudd suddenly shrieked with joy!

"*Flamenco!*" she screamed. "*Flamenco!*"

She cast aside poor, bewildered Lenny in the hall and grabbed one of the lacy, silky, red and black dresses. The acres of colourful material billowed out as she swung it round the room, stamping her feet and moving her head sharply from side to side, with a look of thunder in her eyes.

Lenny quickly changed the record and all at once the house was filled with the passionate, dramatic music of the Spanish gypsy dance, the flamenco!

Then, to the intense rhythm, he, too, started banging his feet crazily on the floor tiles in the kitchen, his face like thunder as well! Then he started waving his arms about, and grabbed the tea-cosy off the tea-pot on the kitchen table and plonked it on his head!

They started moving towards one another, still madly banging their feet, and glaring at one another with angry eyes. Lenny crazily moved his black, bushy eyebrows up and down and then started moving around Rita who'd sank dramatically onto the hall carpet. On and on he went, and then he too, finally collapsed in a heap on the floor amid the billowing dress and a shout of "O-ley!!"

The performance was greeted with wild applause from Roberta and Maxwell, although they both looked a touch embarrassed.

"*Bravo, senor and senorita*!! More! More!" called Robbie.

"I'm shattered!" gasped Lenny. "The flamenco is even more tiring than the tango! We'll try again when we've demolished the fish 'n' chips!"

Of course, the twins remained as snooty as usual.

"We'll show you how to do the flamenco after tea!" Daffodil announced rather haughtily. "It's in our blood! We were born to dance!"

"I wish our two were!" panted Rita, looking up at Roberta and Maxwell. "They've both got two left feet! But they're beginning to show a bit of promise! We'll make champions out of 'em someday!"

During tea, Mrs Nudd was quite in awe of the two flowery-dressed young guests, especially when she discovered their wonderful names and talked about their dancing and their trips to Spain! The twins politely nibbled at their fish and chips.

"I wish I'd named *you* after a flower!" she said, as she made herself a chip sandwich to finish her meal and looked at her green headed daughter across the table.

"Crocus...or Hyacinth...or Bluebell!" she continued dreamily. "Even Rose or Heather would have been better than *Roberta*! I don't know what possessed me!"

"Take no notice of your mum, Robbie!" said Lenny, giving her a hug. "I think you've got a lovely name! I wouldn't have m' little princess called anything else!"

By now Roberta was absolutely seething inside, and kept looking at the kitchen clock, wishing that time would fly as it had never flown before! It was still only just gone seven o'clock and the twins' chauffeur wouldn't be arriving until eight!

Then to make matters worse, more dancing followed tea, and soon she had to put up with the twins not only showing off their flamenco, but then *Honeysuckle dancing with Maxwell* while she danced with Daffodil!

What a nightmare, as she watched the tall, dark, olive-skinned girl getting closer and closer to her beloved Ozzie! Her hands were everywhere!

And when, during a very dramatic part of the dance, their faces almost touched...well, that was the last straw! Robbie, in one superb bit of footwork, dropped Daffodil in a heap, bulldozed Honeysuckle out of the way and grabbed Maxwell in her arms.

"*Roberta*!" shouted her mother. "What a terrible way to treat out guests! You should be ashamed of yourself!"

Robbie smiled sweetly and swept Maxwell round the room...the poor, bewildered boy totally unaware of the powers of the green-eyed monster burning fiercely within his green-haired girlfriend!

Strangely, Honeysuckle just looked at her sister and winked. And then she put her thumbs up as though some cunning plot was working very well.

If only Maxwell had realised what had just happened as he'd danced with the girl with the golden feet! But he hadn't noticed that, while he was trapped in her passionate arms, something very precious had been taken from the back pocket of jeans. Something very precious indeed!

At exactly eight o'clock the chauffeur peeped the raspberry Ferrari's horn and the twins gathered up the flamenco dresses and headed down the hall.

As Lenny politely opened the door, and to the complete surprise of everyone, the twins suddenly announced that it was their birthday in just two days time...on the Thursday! They would be eleven.

And then, even more surprisingly...they invited Rita and Lenny and Roberta and Maxwell to the party!

"It will be wonderful!" boasted Daffodil, taking one last look at the ghastly surroundings she had just put up with for two hours.

"It'll be absolutely divine!" echoed Honeysuckle, flashing her eyes at Maxwell. "Treat the invitation as a thankyou for the delights of this evening...especially the delightful fish and chips in the newspaper!"

The twins glanced at one another again with that familiar slug-on-lettuce-leaf look.

"And you will be able to see our wonderful mansion and taste our exquisite food!" carried on Daffodil snootily, her nose so far up in the air it was almost touching the hall ceiling!

"Here are the invitations!" said Honeysuckle fishing in her flowery handbag, and producing four silver edged pink invitation cards.

"Midnight, Wednesday!" she went on. "And it's fancy dress! Sorry about the short notice...but try and come in something appropriate!"

"And a small gift for each of us would be appreciated!" finished Daffodil.

"Midnight, remember...the address is on the cards! Mummy's apparently organising the biggest, most fantastic surprise *ever*! So it will be well worth you coming, even if it's just to see how the other half live!!"

And with that, the twins climbed into the raspberry sports car and were whisked away into the night.
The Nudds and the Underdowns looked at one another in amazement.
The early hours of Thursday morning would certainly be interesting!
Very interesting indeed!
But there was still the whole of *Wednesday* to come!
And not to be outdone, that day too, was going to have its moments!

Chapter 13

Honeysuckle and Daffodil were almost the first children on the school playground on a rather grey, overcast Wednesday morning. As they wandered among the giant chesspieces on the giant chessboard, they were deep in conversation like a couple of conspirators. In Daffodil's hand was an envelope...a long, white envelope.

At about half-past-eight, a red post-van pulled up at the front of the school and a cheerful postman dashed across the playground to the school's front door.

"Look's like rain, kids!" he called with a smile to a bunch of children around the climbing frame.

He shoved a bundle of letters into the letterbox, jogged back to his van and drove off.

A couple of seconds later, as Honeysuckle watched to make sure the coast was clear, Daffodil popped the white envelope through the letterbox to join the rest of the morning post.

As they strolled casually back to the chessboard they smiled, raised their arms and celebrated with high-fives!

Another mission accomplished!

By nine o'clock, the yard was packed with children. And, exactly on the hour, one of the Class 4 boys rang the bronze hand-bell that began the school day. The pupils filed in orderly fashion through the doors and into the classrooms, hanging up their coats and bags on hooks that ran down the length of each room.

It was just as Maxwell was putting his duffel coat on his hook, that he felt his back pocket to check the key to the stage-door was there. Suddenly, his heart started pounding and a look of horror crossed his face.

"Robbie!" he whispered. "I can't find the key to the squibbitz! I didn't give it to you, did I?"

"No, *I* haven't got it! *You* always keep it! You haven't changed your jeans, have you?"

Maxwell shook his head and looked puzzled.

"I know it was there last thing yesterday afternoon at school!" he whispered. "I remember checking!"

"Perhaps it's just dropped out at home! We'll pop back to No.34 at lunch time. I'm sure Miss Teezil won't mind!"

"*Buenos dias!*" suddenly chorused Honeysuckle and Daffodil from nowhere.

Roberta cringed. She'd hoped the terrible twosome might be having a day off school to prepare for the social event of the century!

"Hi, guys!" she muttered, trying to muster a smile.

"Hello, Maxwell!" said Honeysuckle.

Maxwell said nothing, his mind elsewhere.

"What's the matter, *Senor* Ozzie?" she asked meekly, placing an olive hand on his arm. "You didn't *enjoy* our little, smoochy dance last night?"

Roberta instantly saw red again!

"I'm the only one who calls him *Ozzie!*" she snapped. "And *no one* smooched *anybody*! Get your mitts off him!"

"Now, now, now...what's going on over there?" came the soft tones of Miss Teezil from the front of the classroom. She looked unusually anxious as she sat at her desk reading a letter.

"Can you all line up?" she said quietly. "And we'll go down to the hall for assembly!"

She picked up her huge handbag and led her pupils into the hall, still grasping the letter in her hand.

Her children sat in a couple of straight lines and the headmistress waddled across the hall, up the steps and onto the stage. She sat down at the piano and started to play.

When Grimmage was headmonster, she'd always had to play the most dirgiest of dirges every morning, but since he'd gone, she'd played really cheerful tunes to begin each day.

But today it was all very different!

The music she played was slow and sad.

Very sad.

Gentle, solemn notes filled the air, dripping slowly from the piano, with long doleful gaps between each one.

It was as if someone had died.

By the time all the children had come into the hall with their teachers, the atmosphere was so unhappy and mournful, that it felt more like a funeral was about to take place rather than a morning assembly!

Some of the older children even had tears welling in their eyes.

At last, Miss Teezil's hands stopped playing.

The notes stopped.

The mood had been created.

She stood up and walked slowly to the front of the stage.

"That's a piece of music I like playing at home, not at school," she said solemnly. "It was written by a Russian gentleman called Shostakovitch. It's part of his Second Piano Concerto...and today, I found it very appropriate to play for you!"

The children and teachers all looked at one another, wondering what was coming next.

"You see, children, we have had some very, very sad news!" she went on, taking a piece of white paper off the piano. "Let me read to you what this letter has to say. It is from the County Council Education Department on their specially headed note-paper. I have just received it in this morning's post."

With every pair of eyes in the hall fixed on her, she began.

It was so quiet you could hear a mouse's heartbeat.

"Dear Headmistress," she started in the saddest voice the children had ever heard, "It has suddenly come to our notice that a property developer in the County has been granted planning permission to build a seventy-five acre retail shopping park on the outskirts of Kirkthwaite."

She paused, lowered the paper and looked at the children before her. She took a breath and continued.

"Such a scheme will be of great economic benefit to the community and create nearly two hundred new jobs."

She stopped again and wiped away a tear.

"Sadly," she bravely carried on, "such a development will involve the demolition of part of the cemetery, the Church Hall, three streets of houses and..."

She paused again, hardly able to utter the next words.

"Chestnut...Hill...Junior School!"

There was a collective sigh from all those listening.

She raised her arm, and silence fell.

"Work on the demolition will begin almost forthwith during the Easter vacation, and all pupils will be transferred to 'Bleak Street Primary School' for the commencement of the Summer Term. We apologise for the very short notice, yours sincerely, Chief of Education."

She lowered the letter in dismay.

Almost instantly, there were sounds of sobbing coming from all parts of the hall, together with angry whispers and whimpers.

It was at that very moment that a distant, faint, ghostly whine could be heard.

Silence fell again and the children, staff and Miss Teezil listened.

The sound came again.

Then again, only louder.

A whine, like that of a chained up dog.

Where was it coming from?

Then the ghostly whine changed to a blood-curdling howl...

made by not one phantom dog...but two, three...

and the fearful sound was coming from...

under the school floorboards!

Suddenly, panic began to strike through the school.

The younger ones began to weep and fidget, comforted by their teacher.

Older children jumped to their feet and tried to look down the crack between the floorboards that ran down the centre of the hall.

All at once the eerie noises became even louder and a weird black smoke clouded with shimmering crystal dust began to seep into the hall through the crack.

The pupils, already deeply saddened by the news and now scared by what they could hear and see...began to move towards the back of the hall...totally out of control!

Chaos and pandemonium was about to hit the school!

Panic-stricken children...running frantically, scared stiff, out of the school...was a recipe for disaster. Someone could be injured...or even worse!

"Stop, stop!" called Miss Teezil from the stage. "Calm down, calm down, it will all be alright! Please children, return to your places!"

But it was too late!

Children and staff were beginning to dash to the doors.

And then, things got even worse!

As the phantom howling reached its loudest and scariest from beneath their feet, a great scraping noise came from the stage.

Everyone stopped dead in their tracks and gazed to the front of the hall.

The piano was moving!

Gliding across the stage!

All by itself!

Chapter 14

One of its legs had suddenly lifted up and then the whole piano had skated slowly across the stage on its little castor-wheels!

What, with ghosts beneath...and now a phantom piano...more panic followed and the crush at the doors was becoming serious.

It was Roberta who suddenly shouted at the top of her voice, "It's the trap door! I know what's happening! It's *Grimbag, Grubbage* and *Gutbucket*!! They're trying to scare us to death! Drive us out of the school!"

As the chaos continued at the back of the hall, and teachers tried their best to calm their pupils, Roberta and Maxwell, followed by Honeysuckle and Daffodil...pelted through the mayhem and onto the stage!

"*After them*!" Roberta exclaimed, disappearing through the trap door. The rest followed into the gloom!

Down the steps and past the old squibbit cages under the hall, the four children raced. In the distance they could make out the three unmistakable figures.

Roberta had been right!

The ghostly noises had come from the mouths of the deadly trio!

"Come on, we can catch them!" yelled Roberta, nearly tripping up over two metal canisters that were emitting the black, crystally

smoke that was seeping into the hall.
"And we can find out where their
secret entrance is at the end of the
tunnel!" called Maxwell.
The gruesome trio suddenly stopped
and Gutbucket's voice echoed up the
tunnel,
"We have the key!" he taunted them,
waving it in the air. "Thanks to my
two brave daughters! We'll get those
precious creatures tonight!"

Roberta and Maxwell skidded to a halt and glared daggers at the
terrible twins behind them.
"So you nicked the key last night, did you?" seethed Roberta. "No
doubt when you were dancing with Ozzie? A quick hand in his back
pocket? I should have known we couldn't trust you! Bet you had a
hand in that venomous letter Miss Teezil read out too, didn't you?"

The twins rushed past and pelted down the
passage after their equally nasty father.
"We'll win in the end!" shouted Honeysuckle. "And I never wanted
your long, lanky carrot topped boyfriend in the first place! It was all
part of our plan!"
"Come on!" shouted Maxwell, suddenly angered into action.
"We've got to find that entrance!"

By now, the deadly trio had reached their secret
door and were waiting for the terrible twins to arrive.
"Quickly, quickly, girlssss!" hissed Grimmage, panting in the
passageway and supported by a heaving Grubbage. "If those two
wormsss from the ssschool find our sssecret entrance, we're done for!"
Gutbucket reached down for the hidden lever, pulled it with all his
might and the stone, rectangular door swung open with a deep,
grating noise.
"Come on, come on!" Gutbucket urged his daughters.
"They're catching you up!"
Closer and closer, Maxwell, with his long legs, gained on the twins.
Almost there!

Just another couple of paces!

He'd be able to grab them by their arms!

Suddenly, the twins swerved to the left and vanished into thin air! The secret entrance, just metres from the end of the tunnel and the blocked-up angel gravestone.

"Come on, Robbie! Come on!" yelled Maxwell, looking back into the gloom of the passage. "We've got to get through before they close it!"

But just as he uttered the words, the stone slab swung shut with a thunderous bang!

The rogues had escaped!

"Sorry, Oz!" gasped Roberta, out of breath as she reached the door. "You were all too fast for me! But at least we've found their secret entrance!"

"The question is...," muttered Maxwell, feeling around the edge of the door, "how do we *open* it? They seemed to reach down for some kind of handle near its bottom edge!"

"It's so dark, you can hardly see your hand in front of...!" said Roberta, her hands pawing the gloom like giant butterfly feelers.

"Hang on, hang on! What's this?" burst Maxwell. "There's some kind of long shape here made of stone. I can move it!"

As he pulled it towards him, a large rectangle of the stone wall began to swing away from him. A dank, earthy smell oozed through the crack making them wince. As he carried on pulling, the crack became wider and wider. Soon it was big enough to squeeze through.

"Are you coming with me?" asked Maxwell excitedly, feeling like *Indiana Jones* or *James Bond*. "I'm going to follow them! You go back and help Miss Teezil, if you want. It'll be safer!"

"You must be joking! I wouldn't miss this for the world!" insisted Robbie.

"Accompanying the famous explorer, Sir Edward Maxwell Underdown, on one of his dare-devil expeditions? Chance of a life-time!"

In case they needed to make a quick escape, they left the door open and then cautiously made their way along a rough, rock-strewn path. This passage was even darker than the one under

the school, but somehow seemed wider. Every so often they stopped
and listened for the sound of footsteps or voices in the distance, but
they heard nothing. The deadly trio and the terrible twins seemed to
have vanished without trace!

They ventured on...into the blackness.

"What's that?" Robbie suddenly yelped.

They stopped and listened.

"Bats!" laughed Maxwell. "You can just hear
their wings beating!"

"Bats! I hate bats!" squealed Robbie,
beginning to wish she'd headed back to the
school. "If one gets stuck in my hair, I'll
scream the place down!"

Maxwell stopped abruptly causing Roberta to
crash straight into him.

"Sorry 'bout that, Rob! Look ahead!" he
whispered. "I can see light!"

Straight ahead, a flickering, orangy glow
seemed to be coming from the rocky walls themselves. As they
walked on, the light became brighter, until they could just make out
the end of their passage. It seemed to be joining onto another, much
larger one!

A kind of subterranean junction!

Then, amazingly, they saw what was glowing!

A torch!

Not an electric torch with batteries, you understand, but a torch of
fire and flames!

Like one in a medieval castle!

"Wowee! Look at that!" Maxwell gasped. "It's like being in the
dungeons under the Tower of London! It's fantastic!"

"Let's just hope we don't meet the ghosts of any headless kings and
queens then!" smiled Roberta, relieved at last at being able to see
where she was!

A moment later they were standing by the torch at the junction. Its
warmth and light were welcome in the cold, dripping cavern.

It was then that they noticed the rails on the floor of the larger tunnel.

A pair of rusty rails, joined together by ancient wooden sleepers.

"It must be some kind of mine!" suggested Maxwell, bending down to inspect them. "And look! Those going in one direction are shinier than the ones leading the other way!"

"As if *those* have been used recently, and *those* haven't!" ventured Roberta, joining in the detective work.

"I reckon our devious little friends have gone *that* way!" said Maxwell, pointing along the shiny tracks. "But they'll be back soon with that key! I only hope that Miss Teezil remembers to put the piano leg back on the trap door!"

"But if she does, that means we're stuck down here, too!" said Roberta. "Unless we clear away all the rock rubble behind the angel door into the graveyard!"

"Right, then we'd better explore sharpish!" said Maxwell.

"I reckon the shiny route could be miles long. Let's try the rusty route! I've got a hunch that it's shorter."

And he was right!

It lead just a few metres and came to an abrupt end...the high, wide tunnel blocked by a dozen or more, thick, vertical beams of wood

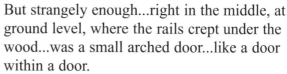

joined together like a solid wall.

But strangely enough...right in the middle, at ground level, where the rails crept under the wood...was a small arched door...like a door within a door.

There was even a handle.

"How peculiar!" whispered Roberta.

"I wonder what's on the other side!"

"Could be just miles and miles of more tunnel!" replied Maxwell, trying to turn the door handle. But it was stuck fast.

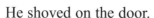

He shoved on the door.

Amazingly, it seemed to budge.

"Come on, Robbie, push! We can get through, I'm sure!"

They pushed again and again...and then suddenly, the door flew open, taking the children with it!
They tumbled to the ground...

and then gazed upwards...

...and they just could not possibly believe what met their eyes!

What lay before them was absolutely *incredible*!!

Chapter 15

Back at Chestnut Hill, the unflappable Miss Teezil was almost ready for take off...her legendary calmness in a crisis being tested to the limit! The letter, the ghostly sounds and the smoke had all had their desired effect...and now every pupil was sitting on the playground in different states of panic and confusion. As a couple of fire-engines screeched to a halt outside the school gates, their screaming sirens adding to the pandemonium, the headmistress tried her best to calm everyone down. But already, alarmed parents were arriving to take their distressed off-spring home, threatening that they would never return.

Then newspaper reporters began to arrive, followed by local radio and television. And when a fleet of ambulances could be seen making their way through the gathering crowds, and two police helicopters were spotted in the sky, Miss Teezil, at last, came to the end of her tether!

After ringing the Education Authority to confirm the news in the letter, she quickly found the sports-day megaphone in the staff-room and headed for the playground, steam almost hissing from her ears.

She stood on the front steps of the school, calmed herself down, cleared her throat and then addressed the chaotic crowd.

"Ladies and gentlemen," she began, her voice booming around the playground and beyond, "children, parents, friends of the school and the brave men amd women who work for our wonderful emergency services..."

The hustle and bustle began to slow down and a hush descended on the chaos.

"Our school today has, in a few short minutes, been the victim of several malicious hoaxes and pranks designed to create the pandemonium you have just witnessed!"

Children, parents, reporters, TV crews all looked at one another with looks of wonder on their faces. It reminded them of all that nonsense that had happened at the school just before Christmas when the Hollywood star Leonora Divine was going to introduce '*the Discovery of the Century*' to a world-wide television audience! That had all ended like a damp squib or a false-alarm!

Now the same thing was happening all over again...but this time, there seemed to be a certain feeling of relief in the air!

Miss Teezil continued, feeling a little more confident. She was, at last, getting things under control like she always did.

"May I make it clear to you all, absolutely crystal clear, that the school is *not*, I repeat, *not*, to be demolished...and neither, may I add, are three adjacent streets, the Church Hall and part of the cemetery! It was all an elaborate hoax conjured up by some evil plotter who seems to have a grudge against the school. The police will no doubt discover his or her identity during the coming days and weeks!"

The headmistress now felt confident enough to switch off the megaphone.

She looked at her pupils scattered around the playground and smiled. Then she took the letter, tore it into shreds and scattered it on the school steps.

"And can I say to you all, my wonderful children," she continued, in her usual voice, "there are *no ghosts under the school* and *Chestnut Hill is not on fire*! It was all part of the hoax...to frighten you all! It's over now, so we can all quietly go back into our beautiful school!"

"Three cheers for Chestnut Hill!" a parent suddenly called from the playground. "Hip, hip...!"

"*Hooray*!!" chorused the crowd.

"Hip, hip...!"

"*Hooray*!!"

"Hip, hip...!"

"*Hooray*!!"

Meanwhile, as the cheering faded and the children made their way back into school, Roberta and Maxwell had begun to explore the strange world through the subterranean door. They had incredibly and totally unexpectedly, stumbled from a dark tunnel into the open air!

They were outside, with the grey Wednesday morning sky above them. "Kirkthwaite folk call it '*The Forbidden Triangle*' or '*The Devil's Back Garden*'!" shouted Roberta over the noise of cars and lorries, as they walked gingerly along the rusty railway track. "Nobody comes here. They say that the air and land are poisonous! There's no life here at all!"

The door had opened onto a vast chunk of land bounded on three sides by traffic filled motorways and dominated by huge, concrete and brick industrial buildings.

The dark, drizzly sky seemed to be held up by dozens of tall, slender chimneys, most of which were pouring out great plumes of thick, black smoke. In one corner were three enormously wide chimneys pumping huge, woolly, billowing, white vapoury clouds into the air. "I used to think it was a cloud factory!" called Roberta. "But it's a power-station making electricity for the whole of Yorkshire!"

The smells were gradually becoming stronger and stronger as they

 wafted around over the poisoned landscape.

"That's a sewage treatment works over there!" pointed out Robbie. "And that's a gi-normous land-fill site for rubbish!"

As they held their hands over their noses, they could see the great, circular sewage treatment beds and bulldozers pushing more and more junk down the sides of a mountain of rubbish.

"Then there's a chemical factory making plastic out of oil!" pointed Robbie. "And a recycling plant!"

The noise that filled the poisonous triangle was almost deafening. The motorways that intersected around the buildings, making the triangle, were full of rush hour traffic, every engine pumping out even more poison into the atmosphere.

"No wonder no one comes here!" shouted Maxwell above the din.

"Yeah! It's a real *no-go area*!" replied Robbie. "It's like hell on earth! Come on, I think we'd better get back through the door! We'll be dead ourselves if we stay here much longer!"

They turned and walked back along the old track, bordered by all kinds of ancient rubbish and dead, leafless bushes and brown grass. It was just after Maxwell kicked an old, rusty watering-can that something caught his eye.

"Wow! Did you see *that*?" he gasped, staring into a small hole by the side of the track in a bank of dead grass. "I can't believe it! No, it can't have been!"

"What?" coughed Robbie, looking into the hole...about the size of a rabbit hole...under a mass of dried up twigs belonging to a dead hawthorn bush.

"It was an animal! It just darted from nowhere and belted into that hole!

And it looked like...a squibbit!! Big hind feet, curly bushy tail, head like a rabbit, great big lop ears!"

"You're joking!" coughed Robbie.

"Surely one couldn't have followed us here from school!"

Suddenly another one appeared on the track!

Then another and another!

Each hopping on their big back feet and gripping in their mouths or in their front paws...a piece of rubbish! Two white plastic milk containers and an old, grubby green towel!!

The children looked at one another speechlessly.

Wild squibbitz!!

And amazingly, they seemed quite tame!

Maxwell bent down and offered, at arm's length, a dried up, old paint-tin, as though he was feeding squirrels in a park!

A moment later there were half-a-dozen more hopping around the children. They offered them anything they could lay their hands on...and each morsel was taken without a hint of fear.

It was incredible!

They were just the same as the captive ones back in the school-house! Maxwell was almost expecting one of them to say *"Thanks, mate!"* or *"I'm a good boy!"*

"I reckon this is where Grimmage and Grubbage got the ones at school!!" said Robbie above the din of the traffic. "They must have come down here, discovered the door..."

"...And then led them back up the tunnels to school with a trail of rubbish!" continued Maxwell. "and then stuck them in those terrible cages!"

"Wow! They must have thought they were on to a fortune! A brand new species of animal, and a rubbish eating pet!" coughed Roberta.

"And then when they found out they could be taught to speak!!" gasped Maxwell. "The dollar signs must have been spinning in their eyes. They must have thought they were onto millions and millions!"

"And here, right beneath the school...was a secret, never-ending supply!" said Roberta. "Plus the ones they bred in the cages!"

"But it's such a dangerous place to live!" spluttered Maxwell. "How do they survive?"

"Well they seem happy enough! All shiny fur, bright eyed and bushy tailed!" smiled Roberta. "You know, I think these are happier here than the ones upstairs in the school-house! After all, they've got all the food they could wish for..."

"And no interfering humans!!" added Maxwell.

As the squibbitz darted in and out of the hole, the children spotted even more of the wonderful animals popping in and out of even more holes scattered all over the barren landscape. At last they tore themselves away from the happy scene, and as it started to rain they left '*The Forbidden Triangle*' determined to keep its strange but enchanting secret.

"The one thing that puzzles me, though," said Roberta as they reached the door and glanced back at the squibbitz, "is why haven't Grimmage and Grubbage helped themselves to *more* of them since they were chucked out of Chestnut Hill?"

"Perhaps it took them years to train the captive ones to speak!" suggested Maxwell. "And that's what they want to do again! Mark my words, it's only a question of time before they start taking this lot! But first...they're determined to grab the trained ones upstairs!"

They stepped through the open doorway and then pulled it shut behind them. The poisoned, noisy secret world was suddenly replaced by the gloomy, dark silence of the tunnel, only lit by the glow of the flickering, flaming torch.

As they paused for a second to let their eyes get used to the light...

...they both heard a sound they'd never heard before...

...a distant rumble...

...from the depths of the black tunnel with the shiny rails...

...louder and louder, closer and closer!

Then...they *felt it*!!

The rusty rails beneath their feet were vibrating!

Shaking!

Something was on the rails!

Travelling towards them out of the dark!

The rumbling almost turned into thunder as the creature closed in on its prey!

The shaking rails began to shake the wooden sleepers and the gravel beneath them!

The two children stood there...

     ...glued to the spot...

...helpless to move!

Chapter 16

A moment later, the rumbling creature of the dark underworld took shape in the orange glow of the torch's flames. It seemed to be slowing down, and the children could see the silhouettes of two figures bending up and down in turn, working some kind of pump. Roberta and Maxwell gazed in amazement along the tunnel.

It was certainly no creature!

More like some kind of weird mechanical contraption that travelled along the rails on four wheels, one at each corner of a wooden platform...its movement controlled by the passengers pumping away on top.

"It must be Grimmage and Grubbage!" whispered Roberta.

"And they're on some sort of miners' tramway trolley that works by muscle power instead of having an engine!"

"They must be going back to the school with the key to the squibbitz, probably thinking the place is deserted!" said Maxwell.

The trolley shuddered to a halt at the end of the shiny rails beneath the torch. The rumbling and the shaking stopped and, once again, all was quiet. The two dark figures jumped off and crunched onto the gravel. Then they reached for a couple of small wire-mesh boxes next to the pump.

"They've got *cages*! Those horrible ones with the sprung trap doors!"

gasped Roberta, looking in horror at the dark shapes of Grimmage and Grubbage. "And they're coming *this way*! Quick, hide!"

As the footsteps crunched towards them, the children squeezed into a couple of shallow crevices in the side of the tunnel and held their breaths.

Closer and closer, their arch enemies marched along the track. Maxwell and Roberta flattened themselves against the rocky walls, their hearts pounding in their ears!

A moment later, the two familiar hideous shapes of Grimmage and Grubbage were level with them...and then they vanished from view. They had arrived at the strange door within a door.

The children just about dared breathe out and peek from their crevices. Grimmage shoved on the door and it swung open.

Instantly, the noise of the motorways broke the deathly silence and the pungent, sulphurous odours drifted into the tunnel.

"Quick, let's follow 'em and see what they're up to!" mouthed Maxwell against the din and pointing at the open doorway.

As Grimmage and Grubbage stepped into *The Devil's Back Garden*, the children stepped from their hiding places and crept towards the grey daylight.

But just as they were about to follow the two rogues into the poisonous wilderness, they both felt the same sudden, excruciating pain at the back of their necks, as claw-like fingertips dug into their skin!

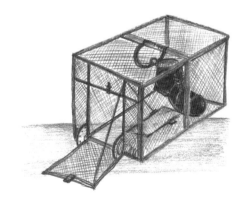

"So what have we here?" growled a menacing voice in their ears, as the vice-like grip tightened.

"Move forward and keep your lips buttoned, you dashed nuisances!

Thought you'd play amateur detectives, eh? Well, I'll teach you to keep your meddling noses out of our business!"

Roberta and Maxwell were helpless to resist as they were driven forwards, the pain throbbing in their necks.

They hadn't noticed the third passenger on the trolley.

A certain Mr Titus Gutbucket.

"Tried to ruin everything, haven't you?" he seethed through clenched jaws, as he pushed his captives along the rusty tracks. "Well, my friends, I think you will see that it is *I* who have the last laugh!"

Maxwell struggled to free himself, but Gutbucket's grip was like iron. "Let Robbie go!" he shouted, trying to twist his head round to face his captor. "She won't go anywhere!"

"No chance of that, my friend! Having you two in our hands is a bonus! You can save us a lot of time and trouble...if you just do what you are told!"

"We'll *never* help you, Gutbucket!" cried Roberta, wriggling and attempting to kick his pink shins. "You'll *never* get your hands on those wonderful creatures!"

It was at that moment that the heads of Grimmage and Grubbage sprung round and set their beady eyes upon their unexpected guests.

"Ahh! We meet once again, you wormsss!" hissed Grimmage, above the noise of the traffic. "Well caught, Mr Gutbucket!"

He then beckoned to the children with a crooked, bony finger.

Gutbucket shuffled them forward, still grasping their necks.

Grimmage dropped the cage he was carrying, darted behind a thorny tangle of twigs and produced another, identical cage...

but this time...containing a cowering, quivering squibbit and a chewed up plastic bleach bottle!

The children were horrified!

"You cruel monster!" cried Roberta. "Leave them alone!"

A wicked smile broke out on Grimmage's face, as he beckoned the children nearer.

Feelings of anger and sorrow brewed and bubbled in their minds as they saw over twenty similar cages each holding a sad, curled up, droop-eared squibbit.

Grubbage rubbed her fat little hands with glee.

"Our fortune assured!" she smiled, glaring at the children. "And this time *you* won't stop us!"

"Don't be so sure of that!" yelled Roberta. "We know what you're up to...and we've got a pretty good idea that you want to introduce the world to these brilliant animals at midnight tonight! At the birthday party of those little brats, Honeysuckle and Daffodil!"

"Ahh! You've guessed correctly!" came the voice of the ice cold grip behind them. "Well done! Yes, those two '*little brats*', as you call them, are my sweet daughters, the apples of my eye!"

"And very good sssecret agentsss and ssspiesss!" hissed Grimmage. "They did very well indeed, ssstealing the key and posssting the letter! Did you find them charming?"

"As charming as...!" burst Roberta.

"Careful, careful, young lady!" growled Gutbucket, sinking his fingers further into the back of Robbie's neck. "We don't want any more bad feeling than is necessary! After all, they *did* invite *you and your parents* to their party, I believe! And I'm sure you would like to be there when we introduce to the world these little furry friends...or rather, their talkative relations upstairs...!"

"And, of coursse, our extra-ssspecial little guessst!" croaked Grimmage, vanishing for a moment behind the decaying trunk of a fallen tree next to a vast, foul looking, black, oozing, stinking bog. He re-appeared with another of those toothless grins etched across his hideous face and his arms behind his back.

Roberta and Maxwell gazed at him, wondering what on earth he was going to show them!

Then, slowly but surely, Grimmage produced yet another cage, but slightly larger than the others.

In it was a heap of rubbish...papercups, an old boot, a couple of paperback books and a lavatory brush.

He lifted the cage to his face and shook it.

"Come on, my little friend, don't be ssshy!" he hissed.

He shook the cage again, this time a little more vigorously.

And then...

...to the total amazement of the two children...and Titus Gutbucket... a creature's head appeared just above the old boot.

It looked like a large mouse...or a rat...black in colour, black beady eyed... with quivering black whiskers.

It looked around, sniffed the pungent air, and then suddenly jumped over the boot to the very front of the cage.

The children nearly jumped out of their skins...and were completely gob-smacked by the creature before them!

It was another cross-breed!

This time, not a cross between a rabbit and a squirrel...but, believe it or not...a cross between a *rat* and a *hedgehog*!!

A rat's head and long tail, but with a body covered in long, sharp spikes or quills, all smoothed down and pointing backwards. Longer spikes than a hedgehog, almost those of a small porcupine!

It was incredible!

Grimmage rapped the cage bars with his white, bony knuckles. Instantly the spikes all stood erect making the animal look like a giant pin-cushion with a head and a tail! The spines quivered and

RAT-HOG

knocked against one another as though in a breeze, making the sound of a rattlesnake. It sounded fearsome, as if it was about to attack!

Grimmage rapped the bars again.

And then came the party trick!

In a flash the strange creature rolled itself into a large, spiky ball!!

The rat's head and tail were gone and all that could be seen was a ball of impenetrable, sharp quills. An armour-coated black rat!!

Grimmage and Grubbage looked at it with a certain amount of pride, as though they themselves had created it.

"It is the forty-ninth that we have trapped since Christmas!" said Grubbage proudly. "The rest are back at Murkbog, upstairs where they are safe from prying eyes!"

"Y...you m...mean, everytime I've visited you this year, you've had dozens of th...those th...things in the upstairs room!" quivered Gutbucket.

"They are our next little ssspecial project!" said Grimmage with a toothy grin. "We are experimenting with parrots to see if *they* can talk, too!"

Suddenly, Gutbucket let out a scream of despair.

"Honeysuckle and Daffodil! They're waiting for me at Murkbog now! If they wander upstairs...! Come on, we've got to get back! What are we going to do with these two nuisances?"

"The appearance of thessse little wormsss hasss opened up a whole new opportunity!" hissed Grimmage, returning the fearsome rat-hog to behind the fallen tree trunk. "We take the girl to Murkbog Towersss as hossstage...and the boy meetsss us with all my furry little darling creaturesss from Chessstnut Hill at, say, two o'clock this afternoon in the cemetery...at the angel gravessstone! We'll meet him there with a large van!"

"But that's *kidnap!*" protested Maxwell.

"No, my boy! That's brilliance! Geniusss!" hissed Grimmage. "No little creatures at two thisss afternoon...no Missss Roberta Nudd! Got it, worm?"

"But the angel gravestone entrance is blocked up!" argued Maxwell.

"*You* blocked it! You *unblock* it!" growled Gutbucket. "Right, let's get going!"

"Take *me* and leave Robbie!" demanded Maxwell.

"She'll never clear the rocks behind the angel!" replied Gutbucket. "She's only the size of a shrimp. You look as though you've got a muscle or two! Come on, no more delays! Let's see some action! The clock's ticking away! It'll be two o'clock in no time!"

Five minutes later, *The Forbidden Triangle* had been left far behind, as the three rogues and Robbie and Ozzie reached the miners' trolley at the tunnel junction.

"Don't worry, I'll be alright!" whispered Roberta to Maxwell in the fiery light, as she was tied to a heavy iron beam on the truck with a piece of rope.

"That's what *you* think!" laughed Gutbucket. "Just wait until you get to Grimmage's place! It's like the House of Horrors!! You'll begin to wish you'd stayed at home and played with your dolls!"

"We'll beat you in the end!" called Maxwell from beneath the torch. "You're no match for *us two!* We've done it *once,* we can do it *again!* The squibbitz will *never be yours!!*"

When a few squibbit cages had been loaded, Grimmage and Grubbage took their positions on the weird lever, see-saw arrangement in the middle of the trolley. Gutbucket squatted down behind the cages and kept his eye on the hostage.
"One, two, three!" called Grimmage at last.
He pushed down his side of the see-saw and the strange vehicle began to inch forwards as he bent his knees. Then Grubbage, with all

her might, pushed her side down. As she bent down, Grimmage straightened up. Up and down, up and down! The vehicle picked up speed and began to rumble along the tracks.
"Bye, Robbie! Good luck!" called Maxwell, as the truck faded into the dark and then vanished around a corner.
The noise drowned out his words.

Roberta gazed into the blackness and wondered what lay ahead. She shivered in the cold breeze and thoughts of rat-hogs, the House of Horrors and meeting the terrible twins again flashed through her mind.
Had she bitten off more than she could chew this time?
Would she ever see Chestnut Hill again?
Miss Teezil?
Would she ever see No.34 again?
Her mum and Lenny?
Would she ever see Maxwell again?
A single tear-drop trickled down her cheek and was blown away on the cold breeze.

Chapter 17

The truck rolled on and on into the unknown...

....and so did Roberta!

Maxwell reckoned that if Miss Teezil had managed to steady the ship and get the school back to normal, then it must be around morning play-time by now. He had about three hours to unblock the door in the angel gravestone and then fetch the squibbitz from the school-house. When he reached the passageway that led to the cemetery he headed down to the obstructed doorway. He stood in the darkness and gazed unhappily at the task ahead.

It was going to take ages!

There must have been fifty or even sixty chunks of solid rock to move!

He and Robbie had certainly made a good job of blocking it up!

By the time he'd shifted a dozen he was shattered. Sweat was pouring off his forehead and his legs felt like jelly. He sat down and rested.

He'd been at it for at least half-an-hour and he'd only moved a quarter of the stones.

He felt heartbroken. The task was impossible!!

He was going to let Roberta down!

He took a deep breath and carried on.

Another three, four, five, six...

...he stopped again, panting hard.

Suddenly...he heard a sound amid the thudding of the heartbeat in his ears.

Footsteps.

Fast footsteps!

Was he imagining them?

He listened.

Then he made out a beam of white light from a torch bouncing around, further up the tunnel.

Who could it be?

Friend or foe?

He decided to hide amongst the rocks and keep quiet.

The footsteps became louder and louder.

Suddenly, the torch beam picked him out.

He shielded his eyes against the glare.

"Anyone down there needing a spot of help?" called the familiar voice of...he could hardly believe it...*Miss Teezil*!! "Is that *you*! Maxwell?"

The headmistress had been down the passageway several times with Roberta and Maxwell on exercise trips with the squibbitz. After the events of the morning she'd calmed the school and then asked the Year 3 teacher to look after her class while she set off to find out what had happened to Roberta, Maxwell and the twins.

"I climbed down through the trap door, turned off those awful tanks of smoke and then made my way here!" she said gently, as though she did that sort of thing everyday!

They decided to go ahead with Grimmage's plan in case some harm came to Roberta.

"I'm tempted to have the police waiting in the cemetery when they arrive in their van!" she said angrily. "I'd like to see them *all* behind bars! And the sooner the better! And to think that I was completely fooled by that letter...and those twins!"

But Maxwell persuaded her otherwise.

If some police trap was rumbled by the three rogues, then who knows what could happen to his best friend...the kidnapped hostage!

During the next hour or so, the two of them managed to move all the rocks...and at precisely five minutes to twelve, Maxwell nudged open the angel's door. Fresh air flooded the passageway and the exhausted pair rested.

"I'd love to stay here all day!" exclaimed Miss Teezil, propped up against the tunnel wall. "But I've got to get back upstairs and see to the school. It's dinner-time! Do you want me to get you a helping?"

"No thanks, Miss, there's no time!" said Maxwell. "I've still got to lay a trail of goodies for the squibbitz...to make sure they follow me down the passage!"

"Oh, they will, my boy, they will!" said Miss Teezil getting to her feet. "They'd follow *you* to the ends of the Earth! It makes my blood boil to think that the poor animals are *still* in danger! But mark my words, young man...we'll win the battle! Everything will turn out fine in the end!"

"All's well that ends well!" beamed Maxwell, as they made their way up the dark passageway, but he couldn't help thinking what was happening to Roberta.

The miners' trolley had sped away into the blackness along an almost perfectly straight track with just one large bend. It was marked every so often by flaming torches fixed to the tunnel wall. She'd counted six in all as the clattering wheels on the rails whisked her into an unknown subterranean world.

She'd learned at school that there were ancient lead mines under Kirkthwaite, all carved out by hardy miners in candle-light. Thousands of men had worked in the tunnels and passageways over the centuries, but now the workings lay abandoned. She reckoned that the main tunnel with the track was how the lead was carried to the outside world, probably in little trucks pulled by donkeys or even steam engines. Occasionally she'd noticed smaller tunnels branching off and imagined how tough life must have been for the workers, some of them children.

"Another minute and we'll be there!" called Gutbucket, as Grimmage and Grubbage continued yanking up and down on their see-saw.

After the seventh flaming torch, they stopped, collapsed in a heap and tried to catch their breaths, as the trolley free-wheeled to a halt a few metres from another one sitting on the track.

"One of these days, you'll give us a hand!" grumbled Grubbage to Gutbucket.

"One of these days *I* will have master-minded your fortune!" replied Gutbucket, with an air of superiority. "I don't think it's too much to ask that *you* do the donkey work!"

Gutbucket undid the knot that bound his prisoner to the iron beam, and pointed to a small, arched opening in the tunnel wall lit by another fiery torch. Roberta could just make out two or three rough-cut, rocky steps.

"It's a bit of a climb, but we'll soon be at Murkbog!" said Gutbucket. "You can give us a hand with the cages! May as well make use of you!"

He thrust a couple of cages towards her, each with a captured squibbit quivering in the corner.

She looked at them and felt so, so sorry for them.

They looked petrified.

Innocent, harmless animals torn away from their families, trapped in metal boxes, jostled through a strange, clattering, dark world, and forced by the nasty two-footed ones called humans into an unknown future. Roberta felt she was almost in the same position.

And it was at that moment she resolved to do all she could to free *all* the squibbitz and rat-hogs...and return them to their own world, however grim that seemed to be!

At least it was human-free!

The staircase was a spiral set into the rock. There must have been over two hundred steps taking them ever upwards, lit every twenty or so by a warm, welcoming torch. Gutbucket led the way followed by Roberta and then Grimmage and Grubbage, breathlessly panting.

At last they came to another arched door that led into a gloomy cellar, dripping with damp and decorated with dozens of scattered cushions of moss.

"Dashed nearly there!" gasped Gutbucket, trying his best to sound as fit as a flea, although Roberta had spotted that he was wilting along with everybody else.

In the darkest, furthest corner of the rectangular cellar was another door, matching the rest.

"Welcome to *Murkbog Towersss*, Missss Nudd!" hissed Grimmage in the gloom. "I hope you enjoy your stay!"

Gutbucket pushed open the door and a short flight of stone steps beckoned the party up into the ground floor room. As Roberta stepped back onto the surface of the planet, she couldn't help but gaze around in amazement, relieved at feeling a fresh draught on her face and seeing a glimpse of grey sky through the windows. Her exploring eyes fell upon the round, wooden table with the barley-twist candle sticks, the great fireplace with the nearby piles of sheets, the iron candelabra, still slightly swaying rope ceiling and the three carved chairs with the blue velvet to!" upstairs.

But there was no sign of the terrible twins!

"Honey, Daffy! Where are you?" Gutbucket call you're not playing hide and seek...we've got

It then occured to him that they must eithe spiral staircase that led He quickly opened the front door and sh

No reply.

He then darted across the room to

to the second floor.

"Follow me, young lady!" he snapped at Roberta, still carrying her cages.

Robbie followed him up the darker and darker steps.

By the time she reached the last one it was almost as gloomy as the underground tunnel.

She stepped into the second floor room and immediately noticed that all six windows were boarded up with planks of wood. Hardly a single shaft of daylight could sneak in.

Her eyes quickly adjusted to the dark and she began to see all the cages.

Dozens of them littered all over the dusty, wooden floor...and each occupied by a furry squibbit or a bristly rat-hog. Two parrots were sitting on swinging perches.

It was then that she noticed a sight and heard a sound that would haunt her for many years to come!

A sight and sound that made her want to run, not only back down the staircase to the main room...but back down the long spiral staircase to the miners' tunnel way below!

Her heart began to beat faster and faster.

And so did the heart of Titus Gutbucket.

Half of the cages were empty...holes gnawed into their metal mesh, or their trap doors forced open.

Some of the rat-hogs had escaped!

And the sound was of two sobbing, whimpering children trapped against the wall in the dark by over twenty large rat-hogs, their quills standing straight and rattling...ready to attack!

Chapter 18

The scene was straight out of some spooky, Hollywood horror movie, but with one difference!
This was for real!
There were no computer generated images here!
No actors, no film-set, no cameras!
However weird, the rat-hogs were genuine, living creatures...and they were closing in on two ten year old girls, on the day before their eleventh birthday!
Roberta even felt a tinge of sympathy for them!
Titus Gutbucket inched forwards on the creaking floorboards and tried to calm his daughters.
"Everything'll be fine!" he called shakily above the frightening sound of the rattling quills and the desperate sobbing of the girls.
It was then that he noticed Honeysuckle and Daffodil were each grasping an open bag of cheese and onion crisps and an open packet of chocolate chip cookies.
"You're not telling me you've *brought food up here*!" he seethed.
"The smell of it must have driven 'em bananas! They're used to old shoes, plastic buckets and cardboard boxes!"
Grimmage suddenly appeared from downstairs.
"You're right! Drivesss 'em crazy! They'll do anything to get at it!"
By now the rat-hogs were almost at the feet of the terrified twins.

"Get them back! Get them back!" screamed Honeysuckle, as one particularly big and bold rat-hog nibbled at the toes of her pink shoes. "They're going to eat *us* as well as the crisps and cookies!" yelled Daffodil hysterically.

"Serves you right!" shouted Roberta with a grin across her face.

"Help us! Help us! Don't just stand there!" bawled Honeysuckle, as the big and bold rat-hog starting sniffing her pink socks. "We're going to be *eaten alive*!"

"What do we dashed do, Grimmage?" shouted Gutbucket, grabbing hold of the ex-headmonster's shoulders and shaking him. "You've got to save my daughters! I'll give you anything you...!"

Suddenly the loudest scream you ever heard exploded from the lungs of the desperate Daffodil!

Two of the rat-hogs had reached up and their front paws were resting on her knees, their noses and whiskers were quivering wildly, sensing onion, chocolate, and above all, cheese!

"Scatter the crisps and cookies over them all, and leg it!" burst Roberta, suddenly feeling inexplicable pangs of sympathy for the girls.

In a flash, Honeysuckle and Daffodil did exactly what they'd been told, and amid the chaos of flying fur, curly tails and spiky quills, they pelted through the feeding frenzy, past the spectators and down the steps to safety!

Their living nightmare was over!

Never again would they venture anywhere near anything caged while holding anything edible!

So when Mrs Grubbage, out of the goodness of her heart, tried to comfort the distraught twins by offering them a dry cracker each with a spot of Cheddar cheese, you can probably understand why they screamed yet again and dashed out of the front door and into their father's parked gas-guzzler!

Meanwhile, upstairs, a minor miracle was taking place. Roberta had gently stepped forward towards the madly chomping jaws of the rat-hogs and...to the amazement of Gutbucket and Grimmage...had slowly sat down on the floor.

"I'm going to look after you all!" she whispered so quietly that her captors couldn't hear a word.

The chomping stopped...

and the rat-hogs eyed her...

"You'll soon be back where you belong, instead of in these nasty cages! Just wait until I get back! OK?"

The rat-hogs calmed down and sniffed the air standing up on their hind legs.

Roberta looked at the other cages...the ones with rat-hogs, the ones with squibbitz, the odd ones with colourful parrots and several bigger cages with cloths over them at the back...and promised herself that she would return. She just *had* to put an end to all this nonsense!

Five minutes later, she was blind-folded and led to the gas-guzzler outside. She climbed into the monster and sat next to Honeysuckle and Daffodil, who were still shaking and sobbing from their little nightmare.

"Cheer up, you wormsss!" hissed Roberta in her best Grimmage voice. "You're the most ssspoiled bratsss in the world! I wisssh I could ssshove you both in a cage and sssee how *you* like it!"

The twins didn't reply, nor even thank Roberta for getting them out of their tricky situation.

As their father drove his monstrous tank down the track, they just sat there trembling and snivelling.

Perhaps they'd learned some sort of lesson...or, on the other hand, perhaps not. Time would tell.

At precisely half-past-one, a strawberry and cream Titus Gutbucket Enterprises van left Gutbucket Mansion in the depths of the countryside and headed along the lane towards Kirkthwaite.

At the wheel was Gutbucket. In the back was Roberta, her hands tightly tied together. She sat in a dark corner of the windowless box, as it bounced along feeling like a trapped animal. There was no light except for a dribble coming from a little ventilation hole in the roof.

Grimmage and Grubbage were at Murkbog Towers catching a little beauty sleep before the big party at midnight.

Honeysuckle and Daffodil were preening themselves in front of their pink mirrors in their pink bedrooms, already thinking about what gifts they would receive from all the guests at the 'Do' of the Year.

Mrs Gutbucket...Titania, the glamorous Spanish wife of Titus...was downstairs in the Grand Dining Hall with an army of servants, party-planners and caterers preparing the vast space for the celebrations. Already the place was festooned with luscious, glittering pink paper decorations sweeping from wall to wall, almost hiding six great nets suspended from the high ceiling packed with pink balloons and silver confetti. Below, eight long banqueting tables were packed with silver cutlery, cruets and candle sticks together with hundreds of empty china plates and sparkling wine glasses waiting to be filled to their brims with food and drink. There was still plenty of time, Titania Gutbucket told herself! Nearly ten hours before all the fancy and famous guests from the County would start arriving...the Mayors of all the towns and cities, bishops, lords and ladies, business men, stars of stage and screen, sportsmen...the guest list seemed endless! But she knew that it would all be worth while as a special treat for her darling daughters...as well as putting the Gutbuckets at the very pinnacle of Yorkshire society. Her husband would be the toast of the County, especially when he introduced his 'special surprise'...which even she was in the dark about!

As the van approached Kirkthwaite, Gutbucket banged on the back of the cab.

"Nearly there, Miss Nudd! And remember we don't want any funny business! When we get to the graveyard, and pull up at the angel, I want to see all them critters loaded in one minute flat! Any of your tricks and you've had it! Both you and your boyfriend! Got it?"

Roberta could hear his muffled voice, but didn't reply.

She was beginning to feel a bit groggy and travel sick in the dark.

Gutbucket wasn't the most
considerate of drivers...whipping
around corners like a maniac
and stamping on his brakes.
Roberta had been thrown about
like a sack of potatoes. Again
she felt like a trapped animal,
this time on its way to market.
A couple of minutes later the
van arrived at the cemetery.
Gutbucket slowed down, turned

left through the main gates and drove down a narrow tar-mac avenue
bordered by gravestones, bushes and trees.
He could see the angel in the distance. The splendid marble
memorial with its gracious, outstretched wings was almost in the
centre of the graveyard. As the van rolled closer to the gleaming
white statue, he crossed his fingers hoping that Maxwell was waiting
with a hundred of his little, furry friends.
"A millionaire tomorrow!" he whispered to himself with a grin a mile
wide beneath his handlebar moustache.
But it was then...that he saw it!
"Dash! Dash! Dash! And dash again!" he cursed aloud, his grin
wiped off his face in a split second and his hands gripping the
steering wheel harder and harder with anger.
A funeral!
Next to the angel!
Six shiny black limousines blocking the way!
Dozens of darkly dressed mourners, the vicar and a coffin about to be
lowered into the ground!
He could hardly believe his eyes.
A funeral of all things! At exactly the same place he wanted to
park...and at exactly the same time!
"Dang and blast!" he cursed and pressed as hard as he could on his
horn.
The mournful heads of the sombre gathering sprung round as though
they had coiled springs in their necks. Some of the ladies in their

black hats were looking rather agitated and upset.

The coffin continued to be lowered into the ground as the irate, snowy-haired vicar marched towards the intrusive van.

Titus Gutbucket wound down his window and honked again.

"Have you got no respect at all?" snapped the ruddy faced clergyman. "Don't you realise there's a funeral taking place? We're putting old Mr Jenkins in his final resting place! Can't you see what we're doing, man?"

"I don't care what you're doing!" barked Gutbucket. "I've got important business to attend to! This is a public place! I wasn't expecting a funeral!"

"But this is a cemetery, my man!" argued the exasperated vicar, who was getting ruddier and ruddier by the second. "What do you expect to be happening here? A car-boot sale, perhaps? A cocktail party?

Mark my words, you will pay very heavily for causing the displeasure of Our Lord on High. We are in the garden of his house, the church, you know!

He'll be sending you a message to express his anger!"

"I don't care whose gar...!"

At that very moment, a rough grating sound could be heard coming from the base of the angel statue.

All the heads sprung round again and astonished eyes witnessed the most incredible event any of the gathering had seen in their lives!

The lowest panel of the marble plinth began to slide away to one side...

...then two freckly arms appeared from out of the darkness!

Within seconds, pandemonium hit the quiet, tranquil graveyard!

The women instantly started screaming and dashing for the main gates. The men soon followed...all convinced that the angry message from above had arrived in double-quick time and was in the freckly hands of a corpse that was now rising from its grave!

The dozing drivers of the black limousines were also suddenly alarmed and hastily drove their cars out of the cemetery in great clouds of dust...the last one containing the vicar himself!

As Maxwell emerged completely from the secret doorway, Titus Gutbucket jumped out of his cab, smiled and then burst into laughter.

"You did that dashed brilliantly, my son!" he beamed. "What perfect timing! Got rid of them in a flash! And now the coast is clear!! To business, son! Are you accompanied by your 'special delivery'? My future fortune?"

"Where's Robbie first?" demanded Maxwell.

Gutbucket quickly opened the van's rear door and revealed poor Roberta, crouched at the back, squinting and shielding her eyes in the sudden flood of daylight.

"You monster, Gutbucket!" Maxwell exclaimed, as he looked at his best friend. "How could you treat her like that?"

"Easily, my friend!" smirked Gutbucket. "Now let's get on before there's another funeral!"

He had already spotted a couple of squibbitz just by the marble door, as Maxwell dragged a bulging, black plastic bin-liner out into the open.

"Can I have some food? I'm starving!" squeaked one, as it licked its droopy ears.

"Hello and how are you? I'm very well thankyou!" chirped the other, scratching itself happily.

Gutbucket stared at them with affection.

"Aren't they just wonderful?" he smiled soppily, as Maxwell emptied the contents of the bin-liner on the grass and laid a trail up to a plank which Gutbucket slid down from the back of the van to make a ramp.

Then he pulled out another black bag from the statue and emptied it into the van itself.

"That should keep 'em happy until I get back to the mansion!" said a rather satisfied Gutbucket. "Right now, let's

get the furry, little cuties in with Miss Nudd! Call them will you?"
Roberta reluctantly called for the squibbitz to come out of the
passageway and follow the trail of rubbish into the van.
One after the other, the squibbitz hopped, skipped and jumped into
the vast, dark trap. It looked like a scene from *The Pied Piper*!
When all were settled, nibbling on the rubbish, Gutbucket asked
Maxwell to jump aboard and undo Roberta's hands so she could
climb out.
Willingly, Maxwell clambered into the van while Gutbucket pushed
up the ramp plank after him.
Then, as he began to close the van doors, he slyly cackled,
"Got you, my friend! I think the *two of you* will be very useful back
at *Gutbucket Mansion*! Have a good journey!!"
As the heavy doors clanged shut, Roberta and
Maxwell and a hundred squibbitz were plunged into blackness.
The children had been well and truly tricked and trapped!
The engine coughed into life, and they could feel the van rumbling
through the graveyard.
Maxwell put a comforting arm around Roberta in the shaking,
shuddering dark and they both silently wondered what would happen
to them when they next saw daylight!
What exactly had Gutbucket got in store for them?

But one thing was for sure!
They were determined not to be beaten!
Roberta was already hatching a plan of her own!
She gave Maxwell a peck on the cheek and together they began to
plot and scheme in the blackness, surrounded by their furry, lop-eared
friends.
Soon, *they* would have something in store for *Gutbucket*!
The tables would be turned!
And '*Revenge would be sweet*'!

Chapter 19

As usual, at exactly six o'clock, Mrs Nudd burst through the front door of No.34, Chestnut Terrace.

"Hello, everyone!" she called as she hung her coat up in the hall.

But all was quiet.

"Hello!" she called again.

It was then she heard a familiar sound coming from upstairs!

The *snotty-piggy-foghorn* she had invited to share her house!

Lenny...snoring in the bedroom.

"Lenny, I'm home from work!" she shouted from the bottom of the stairs.

"Nice to see you've made me a cup of tea! Nice to see you've got the evening meal ready!"

Still, the *snotty-piggy-foghorn* continued.

Furiously, Rita charged up the steps, two at a time, nearly knocking her vases of flowers flying...and flew into the bedroom.

She skidded to a halt and gazed at the peaceful sight before her.

Lying on the rose covered bedspread was her beloved Lenny, fast asleep like a baby...lost to the world...a sweet, satisfied smile across his carefree face.

Once again, the *snotty-piggy-foghorn* blasted around the bedroom, almost making the ornaments on the dressing-table and window-sill shake and rattle.

Rita took the deepest breath her lungs would allow and crept over to her sleeping prince.

The *snotty-piggy-foghorn* rumbled again.

She bent forwards and moved her lips towards the mass of ruffled, unkempt black hair that was spread on the rosy pillow.

And before another snore could explode from the bed, she yelled at the top of her voice,

"*LENNY*! *Wake up, you idle...*!"

In a flash of sudden terror, Lenny's eyes shot open and he sat bolt upright as though a thousand watts of electricity had shot through his body!

"Wh...what's the matter, pet?" he mumbled, rubbing his eyes. "Is the place on fire?"

"No, but *I am*!" shouted Rita. "I've been out at work all day! I come home shattered...and what do I find? *You*...snoring your head off! What've you been doing all day? Got yourself a job yet? Made the tea? Vacuumed the house? More like watchin' the telly, fillin' your belly and having a nice afternoon nap!"

The whirlwind of words left Lenny speechless.

He just sat there with his mouth open like a goldfish.

"And the kids! Where are *those two*!" Rita stormed on. "They should be here, ready for tea! Don't tell me they've gone walk-about *again*!!"

Lenny dared a word or two.

"They'll soon be hungry! And they've got to get ready for that party they've been invited to by Snowdrop and Tulip or whatever they were called! They'll be back in no time. You just watch!"

"That's what you said last time...and look what happened! After midnight when they turned up! I tell you, this is the last straw!"

"We'll give 'em till nine," Lenny risked, "and then we'll call the coppers!"

"You must be *joking*!" snapped Rita. "It was so embarrassing last time! And *what* will the neighbours think? The police turning up for the *umpteenth* time! They're going to start thinking this place is a den of criminals!"

Meanwhile, in a real den of criminals, Grimmage and Grubbage were all spruced up, ready for the social occasion of the century...although, to be honest, it was hard to tell! Grimmage was sitting by the fireplace nibbling a custard-cream, having brushed down his one and only suit...the one he had worn day-in and day-out ever since he'd been thrown out of Chestnut Hill. It was full of stains, dribbles and creases...and looked like he'd slept in it for months!

Actually, he had!

It made him look like a complete tramp...unshaven, untidy and a bit smelly!

And Grubbage wasn't much better!

She'd tried her best to keep up some sort of lady-like appearance, but had finally been beaten by the squalour of Murkbog Towers. She was sitting by the table, looking at herself in a cracked hand-mirror.

"Just look at my hair!" she grumbled, pulling her thick fingers through the browny-grey and greasy mop.

"I'd rather not!" cackled Grimmage.

"How can I possibly go to the Gutbuckets' 'do' looking like one of the Ugly Sisters?"

"Gad, my good lady, the Ugly Sssistersss look like beauty queensss compared to you!" hissed Grimmage. "Why don't you put your cook's hat on and cover as much of your head as possssible? You don't want to be ssscaring those two daughtersss of Gutbucket! He'd never forgive you!"

"Well, that's pretty good coming from *you*, I must say!" snapped back Grubbage. "One look at you and you'll empty the place! They'll think someone's dug you up!"

Grimmage looked up from his custard-cream and smiled one of his wicked smiles.

"Remember, it's a *fancccy-dresssss* party!" he hissed, wiping the crumbs from his dribbly chin. "We could come away with the *Firssst Prizzze*!"

By amazing coincidence, just at that very same moment, Mrs Titania Gutbucket was arranging the prizes on a gold covered table at the end of the Grand Dining Hall. She looked extremely elegant in a long, silver ball-gown bedazzled with diamonds. Perched on her immaculately groomed, raven coloured head was a matching, glittering tiara. She looked like the Queen of Spain, never mind the wife of that conniving, scheming, money-grabbing pink rogue who called himself Titus!

By now, the decorations in the Hall were complete and the caterers had done their job, too. The kitchen tables and refrigerators were groaning under the weight of all the prepared food.

Titania looked around and lapped up the wealth and utter luxury on display. The Gutbuckets would *definitely* be the talk of the County after this! She could hardly wait to hob-nob with the rich-and-famous as they arrived in their chauffeur driven Bentleys and Rolls-Royces! Lord and Lady Wensleydale were even coming by helicopter! Fancy that, she thought to herself, a helicopter landing in the grounds carrying Lord and Lady Wensleydale, the poshest folk in the whole of Yorkshire! What a night it was going to be!

Upstairs, on the fifth floor, in their pink bedroom, the spoiled brats known as Honeysuckle and Daffodil were combing each other's cascades of long, black, shimmering hair and gazing into their gilt-edged mirror.

"We *are* beautiful, aren't we?" said Honey, smiling at herself and posing her head from side to side, as though a bunch of phographers were snapping away.

"We *are*! There's no doubt about it!" replied Daffy. "We will be the

belles of the ball! And I can't wait to show off to everyone from Snootem School! It'll be so good to see them again after being at that terribly awful Chestnut dump for two days!"

"I agree!" said Honey. "It felt more like two *years* than two *days*!!"

"Just *imagine... having* to go there *every day*!" said Honeysuckle.

"How *terribly awful*!" agreed Daffodil, also posing for pictures. "No tennis courts, rose gardens or even water fountains! How *terribly awful* for those nasty, little, common children!"

"Especially that streak of a carrot, Maxwell!" added Honey. "And his snitchy shrimp of a girlfriend...that horrid, horrid Roberta! I wonder what they're doing now...*down there*!"

They both stopped grooming one another and looked down their noses towards Gutbucket Mansion's dark, dank, dripping, dismal dungeons.

Their faces collapsed into those familiar 'slug-on-a-lettuce-leaf' expressions...

...and they both tried to guess...

...but, if only they had known what exactly was going on...beneath their *very own feet*, beneath their *very own house*...!!

If only...!!

Chapter 20

By eight o'clock, Maxwell and Roberta had been locked in a small damp, smelly cellar next to Gutbucket's underground car-park for over five hours! They'd been given some cake, biscuits and orange juice 'to keep their strength up' and told to keep quiet until they were needed at around midnight.

Then, according to Gutbucket, the two of them would be in charge of the squibbitz as they followed a trail of junk and rubbish up to a room near the Grand Dining Hall. As the clock struck twelve and a fanfare of trumpets blasted across the Hall, the amazing creatures would be introduced to the assembled guests.

And after that...Titus Gutbucket would be the toast of the County and on his way to becoming a multi-millionaire!

That was the plan...the *official plan*.

The brainchild of Titus Gutbucket himself.

He was determined to make it a fantastic and wonderful success after the complete and total cock-up at Christmas!

This time the world would *see* the brilliant, cute, talking, rubbish eating animals that would be in demand from every corner of the planet...and *he* would be the sole supplier! OK, he'd throw a few crumbs of comfort to Grimmage and Grubbage for all their work...but it would be *he, Titus Octavius* (his parents were wild about the Romans!) *Gutbucket* that would reap the rewards! His fortune would be made!

The world would be his oyster!

He would be invited to *Buckingham Palace* to meet the Queen and to the *White House* to meet the President!

He would become a household name...on the lips of the world!

'Especially if they call the little critters...*Gutbuckets*!' he thought to himself as he relaxed and soaked in his huge pink bath which overflowed with pink soap bubbles and froth. 'Now that *would* be something!'

Way beneath the gurgling, bubbling bath, the stomachs of the hundred squibbitz still locked in the van were also gurgling!

Gurgling with hunger!

They hadn't been fed for hours!

And on top of that, the van was dark and boring!

It wasn't like being in the school-house, with a tree to climb on and autumn leaves to forage in!

The squibbitz were becoming hungry...in fact, ravenous...and they were becoming increasingly fed up of being cooped up in the dismal dark with nowhere to perch.

They began to scratch at the barren floor and sides of the van. Zziffo and one or two others even began to howl.

"What's that?" whispered Maxwell. "It sounds like a cross between a wolf, an owl and a ghost!"

"Perhaps this place is haunted!" whispered Roberta. "Have a look through the window!"

The small cellar had a tiny air vent or glassless window high up above the locked door. Maxwell clambered up onto an old wooden crate and reached up on tip-toes. He peeped through the rough hole which was no bigger than an exercise book.

In the half-light he could make out the rough stone walls of what once had been a series of linked dungeons. Now they had all been knocked into one big space that had become the underground car-park or garage for Gutbucket's fleet of vehicles. He could see the raspberry Ferrari, a couple of pink Rolls-Royces, the monstrous pink gas-guzzler, and the strawberry and cream van at the end of the line. Beyond the van was some sort of mystery vehicle covered in a green tarpaulin.

"I reckon that's *my caravan!*" gasped Maxwell. "It looks about the right size! It'd better be in good nick, or Gutbucket's for it!"

Suddenly, he noticed that the van was gently rocking!

"Robbie, the van we came in is moving from side to side by itself!" whispered Maxwell. "The squibbitz must be up to something! That's where the weird howling's coming from!"

As he watched, the van began rocking even more and the howling became louder and louder!

Suddenly, a door opened at the far end of the underground car-park. Bright light flooded into the dark dungeons and Maxwell could see the shape of a huge, burly, bald-headed giant of a man silhouetted in the doorway, with muscles like melons bursting out of his T-shirt!

"One of Gutbucket's heavies has come to sort out the fuss!" Maxwell whispered. "You should see the size of him! He's built like a battleship!"

The burly giant stomped over to the van and banged the side of it with his sledge-hammer of a fist.

The noise echoed around the dungeon like an explosion.

The howling stopped instantly, and the van stopped rocking.

"You lot be quiet in there!" he thundered.

"You lot be quiet in there!" came a muffled, squeaky reply from inside the van.

The burly giant couldn't believe his ears! He'd been told that there were animals in the van...but not *talking ones*!

Then, a whole chorus of squeaky voices rang in his ears!

"You lot be quiet in there! You lot be quiet in there!"

Suddenly, it occurred to him that there could be people locked inside. Scratching his bald head, he marched down the side of the van, grasped a handle, carefully opened one of the doors...and peered insi..!

BANG!!

The tidal wave of fur, paws, bushy tails and lop-ears hit him like an express train out of a tunnel!

In a split second he was flat on his back, under a stampede of angry squibbitz!

Some nibbled and bit at his clothes and boots, while others sprung onto the raspberry, open-topped Ferrari and started munching its delicious red leather seats and folded up cloth roof, not to mention demolishing a couple of tennis rackets and a whole load of CDs and cassettes!

The car and its contents were wrecked in minutes!

The burly giant struggled to escape and eventually crawled over to the pink gas-guzzler, a dozen squibbitz with clenched jaws hanging onto his trousers. He dragged himself up to its door handle, clambered in and fished about for the ignition key. In seconds the squibbitz were all over the inside of the monstrous vehicle, devouring everything in sight and swinging around the bald head of the panic-stricken driver!

Suddenly, its engine burst into life...the burly giant pressed the accelerator...and the tank shot forwards at top speed with the door still open...

...straight through the wooden

doors of the car-park...

...straight across a beautifully manicured putting-green...

...and straight into an enormous ornamental pond!

S-P-LASH!!

Just before it took off for its perfect dive, a dozen squibbitz flew out of the door along with its driver...and landed on top of the ninth hole, the flag pole spearing the unconscious burly giant in the middle of

his rather ample bottom!!

Slowly, the gas-guzzler sank into the pond amid a flourish of bubbles, until just its roof could be seen as a flat island covered in weeds and lily-pads. A minute later, several ducks were enjoying a new nesting spot!

By now, the rest of the squibbitz in the car-park had climbed all over the Rolls-Royces and found their open windows! In moments, their jaws were chomping on everything they could lay their paws on! And five minutes later, the insides of the cars were completely destroyed, and the squibbitz sat on the two pink roofs burping and scratching themselves contentedly, while their dribbly poo dribbled down over the glossy paintwork!

That was more like it!

Grub and excitement!

Much better than being cooped up in a dark, boring old van!

All through this mayhem, of course, Maxwell had been watching every move and reporting the incredible action to Roberta, who was giggling down below.

"If only we could get out of this cursed cellar!" she burst, sipping the last of her orange juice.

Just then Maxwell spotted Zziffo sitting on the car-park floor, nibbling on a pair of snazzy, red driving gloves he'd pinched from the wrecked Ferrari. He whistled and called,

"Zziffo! Zziffo! Come here!"

Zziffo's droopy ears instantly pricked up and looked up at Maxwell's face peering out of the small window. The squibbit dropped his gloves and in a flash had climbed up the rough stone walls on the outside of the cellar.

The next moment he was sitting on the window ledge, just inches from Maxwell's face.

"Me, Zziffo! How are you?" he squeaked, raising his ears up and down.

"Good boy, Zziffo, good boy!" replied Maxwell, knowing what he had planned was a long-shot...but it might just work!

During visits to the school-house to feed and exercise the squibbitz, Maxwell had shown Zziffo several items and taught him their names.

Already Zziffo could say '*tree*', '*leaf*', '*door*', '*bucket*', '*brush*' and, most importantly, '*key*'!

Normally Maxwell used the key to the school-house door to show Zziffo what one looked like. He'd often played a game where he hid the key under the autumn leaves and asked the squibbit to find it. Maxwell knew there was one in the lock of the cellar door. The question was...could Zziffo get it and bring it up to him? Then, with any luck, they could open the door from the inside!

"Key!" he whispered to the squibbit. "Find *key*! Fetch *key*!" Zziffo looked at him blankly. Perhaps the squibbit was too excited to think about words. Perhaps it would only work in familiar surroundings.

"Key!" Maxwell patiently repeated.

Still, the squibbit looked at him blankly, cocking his head from side to side. Then, suddenly, the penny dropped!

"*Key*!" squeaked Zziffo. "*Key! Key! Key!*"

"Yes, *key*!" gasped Maxwell, astonished at the words bursting out of the furry animal's mouth. "Find *key*! Fetch *key*!"
Instantly, Zziffo turned round on the ledge...and was gone!

Surely the squibbit couldn't possibly return with the key to the door!
It *had* to be a *thousand-to-one* chance!
A *million-to-one* chance!

Roberta and Maxwell looked at one another...
        ...crossed their fingers...
                ...and hoped!!

Chapter 21

"I can hear him! He's climbing up the wall!" whispered Maxwell excitedly. "Keep your fingers crossed, down there!" A moment later he was nose to nose with the squibbit...and amazingly, in his mouth...was a key!!

Admittedly not the *right* key! But it was a key! And a useful key at that!

It fitted in very well with their plans!

Maxwell was absolutely gobsmacked! The squibbit had done exactly what it had been told and fetched a key!

"Well done, Zziffo! Zziffo, good boy!" he praised the wonderful animal.

"Good boy! Good boy!" echoed the squibbit, seemingly delighted that he'd pleased Maxwell.

Gently he took the ignition-key from one of the Rolls-Royces and slipped it into his back pocket.

"Good boy! Good boy, Zziffo!" he repeated. "Find *key*! Fetch *key*!"

In a trice, the squibbit vanished and returned with another key clenched between its long front teeth.

Again Maxwell was gobsmacked!

And this time, even better...it wasn't an ignition-key!

It was a large, ancient looking, iron door key!

But was it the one from their cellar door?

"Good boy, Zziffo! Good boy!" Maxwell beamed, as he once again gently took the key from the squibbit, and passed it down to Roberta. She pushed it into the door's key-hole and tried to twist it, praying that it would work from the inside.

"It's not working! I can't get it to turn!" she said impatiently.

"Keep trying, Robbie! It's *got* to work!"

Suddenly, a loud click echoed around the cellar.

"It's worked! It's worked!" yelled Roberta, turning the brass handle.

At last, the door yawned open with an eerie creak...and the children were free!

Now, the fun could *really* begin!!

Upstairs, as Gutbucket was drying himself off in his luxurious bathroom, he heard a knock on the door.

"Dashed what is it?" he called. "Can't a man have a bit of peace and quiet in his own dashed bathroom?"

"S..sir, it's me, sir! C..Cruncher!" came a deep, but somehow stuttering voice. The burly giant had come round at last on the putting green and had an extremely sore bottom!

"What do you want, man?" snapped Gutbucket. "What are you doing up here?"

"It's the g..garage, s..sir!" dithered Cruncher. "I..I opened the v..van...and...!"

Gutbucket flew to the door, opened it and glared at his bodyguard with a look that could have sunk an aircraft carrier!

"*WHAT*?" he bawled, dropping his pink towel. "*What've you done?*" He didn't wait for an answer.

Instead, completely starkers, he tore straight past Cruncher, across the bedroom, along the corridor and down the first flight of stairs.

On the next landing he met his wife and two daughters, charging like whirlwinds from *their* bedrooms!

On seeing the naked Titus, they screeched to a halt, with a mixture of shock, horror and sheer embarrassment!

"*Father*! Put something on!" chorused Honeysuckle and Daffodil, both blushing bright red, and not knowing whether to cover their eyes or burst into laughter!

Gutbucket grabbed a bunch of flowers to cover his modesty, and rushed down the next flight of stairs followed by Titania, Honey, Daffy and Cruncher with the pink towel.

"Did you hear the noise coming from the kitchen and the Grand Dining Hall?" Titania feverishly gasped.

"What noise?" panted Gutbucket. "What are you talking about, woman? I'm on my way to the dungeons to check the van!"

At the bottom of the stairs, the Gutbucket whirlwind met a whole, panic-stricken wall of servants pelting along the main ground-floor corridor like a stampeding herd of wild wildebeest!

"Don't go *that way*, sir!" exclaimed one of the girls. "It's like feeding time at some crazy *zoo*!"

And indeed it was!

But much, much worse!

The *Pied Pipers*, Maxwell and Roberta, without even a flute or a trail of rubbish, had led all the squibbitz upstairs from the garage into the Grand Dining Hall and the kitchen! The result was complete and utter havoc and devastation! It was as though a terrific, twisting, tornado with teeth had torn through Gutbucket Mansion destroying everything in its path! And by *everything,* boy, do I mean *everything*!

First, the squibbitz had left the Grand Dining Hall totally wrecked! Every single pink, paper festoon ripped from the ceiling, along with the nets of glittering confetti and pink balloons. The squibbitz enjoyed their 'starter course' immensely, especially the popping balloons, garnished with dozens of broken china plates and barley-twist candles, not to mention all the little boats of sauces and dips.

The buffet tables loaded with hundreds of delicate canapes, sausage rolls, sandwiches, olives, cakes and biscuits were all demolished! The cute, furry creatures vacuuming every single tasty morsel down their throats with relish.

Zziffo and ten of his mates attacked the lavishly decorated birthday cake at the end of the Hall and totally wrecked it! What had been a pink fairy castle topped with Spanish dancers became a pile of crumbs in five minutes flat!

Then, as if the starter course wasn't enough, the squibbitz moved on to the kitchens, where the main course offerings were irresistible!

The fridges were prized open to be pillaged and ravaged like a honey bear in a bee-hive or an anteater in a termites' nest. Scrumptious strawberry trifles, apple pies, lemon meringues, Black Forest gateaux, platters of salmon, turkey, duck, ham and roast beef were demolished in seconds, not to mention gallons of cream, horse-radish sauce, mint sauce, bread sauce and ever other kind of sauce you can think of!

It was absolute carnage!

The squibbitz just chomped and burped, munched and burped, chomped and burped, munched and burped...until they were completely full to the brim...hardly capable of moving!

Maxwell and Roberta, of course, enjoyed every single moment of the gorging spectacle and watched as every single mouthful disappeared down the squibbitz' throats! They even treated themselves to the odd tasty chicken drum-stick, a toffee apple each and a mouthful or two of fresh pineapple! It was one heck of a feast! And who could blame them after being imprisoned for hours in that dank, dark cellar?

This was definitely pay-back time!

And they smiled as they imagined the Gutbuckets getting ready for the poshest '*do*' in Yorkshire for *years*! All ready to meet the County's famous and finest!

When the Gutbuckets set eyes on what had happened to the preparations for their little midnight social gathering,

they would be furious!
Maxwell and Roberta wished
they could have hung around
to witness their faces...but
they realised that they had to
evacuate the squibbitz to
safety, before Gutbucket
could get his grubby mitts on
them again!
The question was...*how*?
It was certainly no good

hiding them all somewhere around the mansion until the party was
over. They *had* to get them all off the property *now* and back to
Chestnut Hill, or better still, *Murkbog Towers*! Then they could take
them on the underground railway to the *The Forbidden Triangle*!
There they would be safe from any more human interference and
back in the wild!

The plan they had devised was a brave one...possibly a foolhardy
one...
but they both agreed it was what they *had* to do!
But they had to move quickly!
Very quickly!
The future of the squibbitz was at stake!
They just could not afford to fail!
It was *now* or never!

Chapter 20

At exactly the same moment as the Gutbuckets were tearing along the corridor towards the devastation in the kitchen and the Grand Dining Hall, Maxwell and Roberta plus a hundred squibbitz were just about to make their getaway!

Like a military operation they'd loaded the happy, content and, let's face it, rather well fed squibbitz...into two vehicles in the underground garage.

Half of them into the mystery one under the tarpaulin. (Yes, it *had* been Maxwell's beloved caravan, with all its jungle make-over still in tact! Maxwell just hoped the squibbitz' bellies were full enough for them not to wreck it during the journey it was about to make!)

The other half had been herded into one of the pink Rolls-Royces! The one belonging to the ignition key that Zziffo had obediently brought to Maxwell at the cellar window! Remember?

Things were going well!

Luck had even been on their side! The Rolls-Royce actually *had* a *tow-bar*! Not a permanent one sticking out all the time, you understand! That wouldn't look right on a Roller! Maxwell just had to press a button on the posh walnut dashboard which said '*tow-bar*' and it silently and smoothly glided out from under the rear bumper all by itself!

Brilliant! What engineering!

Now all they needed to do was manoeuvre the pink limousine until they could hook it up to the green caravan!

"Piece of cake!" laughed Maxwell, having driven his dad's Morris on the odd quiet country lane.

Maxwell had started its engine and inched it slowly forwards with ease in the car-park. It was an automatic with no gears to mess about with, so he found it as easy as pie! Being tall really helped, too, as he could reach the two foot pedals with no trouble at all!

Then he put it into reverse and expertly drove it backwards up to his pride and joy!

In a couple of secs they'd hooked them together and were ready for the dash to freedom!

"Now are you *absolutely sure* about this?" asked Roberta, sitting in the squibbit nibbled front passenger seat and hardly being able to see through the windscreen. Behind her, fifty squibbitz were perched on what remained of the rear seat, some snoring away blissfully, some contentedly burping and gazing through the windows and one or two helping themselves to a bottle of whisky from the drinks cabinet!

"No probs at all!" smiled Maxwell. "I've always wanted to do this! Imagine...driving a *Rolls-Royce*!"

Slowly and very gracefully, the poo smeared, pink, luxury limousine crept out of the garage and onto the gravel drive, pulling behind it the ancient caravan. They looked a strange pair! A real odd couple!

"It's so *smooth*!" enthused Maxwell. "And so *quiet*! I can hardly hear the engine!"

He pressed his foot down on the accelerator and the vehicles sped along the drive. The children laughed as they passed Gutbucket's submerged gas-guzzler, still bubbling away in the pond with half a dozen ducks sitting on the roof-island!

Speaking of the Gutbuckets, it was at that very moment that they all stormed into the garage and saw the devastation that had hit their precious vehicles.

"Dang and blast!" cursed Gutbucket, as he tried to console his wife and daughters, who were all in a state of shock having just come from what was left of the Grand Dining Hall and the kitchen. "It's those dashed kids again!"

As he marched grimly out of the garage he noticed his beloved gas-guzzler bubbling in the pond and then saw his Rolls gliding along the drive towards the main gates.

"Dang and blast!" he cursed again, waving a fist.

"I'm not just going to *stand here* and let them walk all over us! I've got to get after the varmints!"

"No time for that, darling!" sighed Titania, gazing through tears down the drive and seeing cars heading towards them. "The first guests are arriving! And look, there's a helicopter hovering in the sky! That'll be Lord and Lady Wensleydale! What on earth are we going to do? A house looking like a hurricane's hit it and not a crumb of food or a drop of drink to give them all! We're going to be the laughing stock of the whole County! And it's all your fault! *Twice* in three months! I tell you Titus, I've had enough! We're through!"

Titania Olivia (*her* parents were wild about Shakespeare!) Gutbucket then took off her wedding ring and threw it at her husband.

"But, darling...!"

"No buts, you fool!" glared his wife. "It's too late! I tell you I've had enough! *We've* had enough! Tomorrow I'm booking a flight to Spain and taking Honey and Daff back to Madrid!"

And with that she stormed back into the mansion, hand in hand with her daughters, and Titus Gutbucket was left to do all the explaining...standing there stark naked, except, of course, for the very well placed bunch of flowers!

Meanwhile, back at No.34, Chestnut Terrace, PC Clegg and WPC Hopkins were standing in the front room.

On the settee Lenny had his arms around Rita who was quietly sobbing.

"I just don't know what's got into them!" she sniffled, dabbing her eyes with a dainty, flowery tissue. "My Roberta's never been like this before! It's all the fault of that son of yours! He's leading her astray! That's what he's doing!"

"Now, now, now, pet!" said Lenny. "I'm sure they'll have a perfectly good explanation when they turn up!"

Just then, the eagled-eyed police lady spotted four pink and silver-lined invitations on the mantelpiece.

"I wonder if *these* may hold the answer!" she said with a grin, as she looked at the address. "Perhaps they've gone there straight after school with...who is it? Ah yes...Honeysuckle and Daffodil *Gutbucket*!! Come on, PC Clegg, I think we've got a party to go to! Have you got the 'cuffs ready?"

Also on their way to Gutbucket Mansion were a certain Mr Grimmage and a certain Mrs Grubbage! They were both sitting in their little car dressed in their finest fancy-dress costumes as it rumbled along the road in the night towards their partner's '*Do*' of the century!

"Can't wait to get there!" said Grubbage excitedly, adjusting her towering cook's hat in the vanity mirror. "I'm absolutely starving!"

"You alwaysss are, my dear!" hissed Grimmage, his bulging eyes staring at the road ahead and his bony hands grasping the steering wheel.

Suddenly he noticed a strange phenomenon heading towards them on the other side of the road. A very strange cocktail of vehicles.

"If I'm not missstaken," he hissed, "isn't that a pink Rollsss-Royce pulling a green caravan?"

Grubbage stopped adjusting her headgear and looked ahead, too.

In a flash the peculiar tandem whooshed past them.

"Wowee! I've never seen anything like *that* before!" she gasped.

"And did you notice the driver? I'm sure I've seen that face before! All gingery and carrotty! I just can't think where! Can you?"

Grimmage shook his head and stared at the road ahead.

"No, I can't sssay that I can!" he replied. "But I'm sure it will come to me...!"

He suddenly turned his head and glared at Mrs Grubbage, and Mrs

Grubbage turned her head and stared at him!

The little car nearly swerved off the road and into the hedge.

"No, it *couldn't* have been!" they chorused nervously. "Could it?"

"No, no, no!" insisted Grimmage, shaking his hideous head once again. "We're letting our imaginationsss run away with usss! There'sss no way that little worm, Maxwell Underpantsss, could *posssssibly* be driving a Rollsss-Royce towing a clapped out old caravan at just after nine o'clock on a Wednesday night! No chance at all! Come on, Mrsss Grubbage, let usss pull ourselves together and get to thisss party!"

By now, of course, Maxwell was having the time of his life...and even Roberta was beginning to feel more confident! Although that was probably because she couldn't see traffic coming in the other direction! Just their headlights!

And...Lady Luck was still with them!

They'd decided that they needed to aim for Murkbog Towers.

The problem was that neither of them knew how to get there!

But once again the buttons on the posh walnut dashboard came to their assistance! This time, the button that said '*Sat Nav*'!

Maxwell pressed it and up popped a little screen just next to the walnut steering wheel.

Roberta typed '*Murkbog Towers*' on the little keyboard...and in a couple of jiffs, a colourful road-map flickered onto the screen with a red, glowing blob of light in the middle following a glowing green dotted road route!

"That's *us*!" Robbie exclaimed. "Look, we're heading towards Kirkthwaite, but we need to take a road that takes us up onto the moors!

You need to take the next turning on the right!"

This was something Maxwell hadn't been looking forward to!

Turning right!

He flashed his indicators and slowed down as he came to the dark junction.

Then he stopped and waited for a car to pass on the other side of the road!

It was then that he noticed what kind of car it was!

Bright fluorescent yellow! *A light flashing on the top*!

A siren making a terrible wailing racket like a cross between a ravenous wolf and some sort of strangulated ghost!

"It's a *police car*!" yelled Maxwell, at last beginning to lose his nerve!

'*Whoooosh*!' it whizzed past in a dazzling white blur of gleaming headlights.

PC Clegg, at the wheel, turned his head and looked at WPC Hopkins and WPC Hopkins turned *her* head and looked at *him*!

The police car nearly swerved off the road and into the hedge!

"No, it *couldn't* have been!" they chorused, suspiciously. "Could it?"

"No, no, no! We're letting our imaginations run away with us!" insisted PC Clegg. "There's no chance a ten year old kid could be driving a Roller...towing a caravan...at this time of night! No chance at all! Come on, WPC Hopkins, let's pull ourselves together and get to this party!"

Maxwell, his heart beating wildly, turned the car off the main road and onto the quieter lane that led to the moors. He slowed down to take a breather.

"Boy, that was a close one!" he panted. "If we'd been spotted, then *that* would have been *that*! The squibbitz would have been discovered!"

"Keep your foot down!" insisted Roberta, looking through the rear window beyond a forest of dozing squibbitz. "If those cops suddenly suspect something fishy's going on, they might be doing one of those screeching U-turns in the middle of the road right now, and coming after us!"

Fortunately, the police car didn't return, and Maxwell enjoyed the rest of his 'chance-of-a-lifetime' ride. And he enjoyed every minute! Incidentally, about a quarter-of-an-hour later, an old Morris passed by the same junction heading for Gutbucket Mansion driven by Lenny, with Rita in the passenger seat...both dressed in their best tango dancing gear, ready to impress the rich and famous! They had a feeling that the police were right...Maxwell and Roberta would be at the party! And, after all, they had invitations, too! So why miss out on a knees-up and a stack of free grub!

As the pink Rolls-Royce's speaking clock announced that it was ten o'clock precisely, the 'Sat Nav' showed the children that the moorland track leading to Murkbog Towers was coming up on the left.
Maxwell slowed down, flashed his indicators again, and turned onto the pot-holed track.
The headlights picked out the great puddles that lay ahead, one after the other, glinting in the moonlight...and with great skill Maxwell steered the car and caravan along the dark, muddy track.
Bump, bump, bump!
Swerving to the left!
Bump, bump, bump!
Swerving to the right!
It seemed never-ending!
But at least the Rolls' fancy suspension made the ride a little easier!
Roberta checked on the fifty squibbitz squashed together in the back.
All were fast asleep, snoring away happily.
She wondered how the ones in the caravan were getting on.
She kept her fingers crossed that they hadn't wrecked Maxwell's pride and joy.
She smiled.
Soon...they'd *all* be *free*!
No more humans!
She couldn't wait!

As they bounced along...the grim, jagged silhouette of Murkbog Towers came into view against the night sky.
It looked lonely and forbidding.
Closer and closer they shuddered and shook.
It was almost like being at sea...in a tiny boat...in a storm!
But, never mind, they'd soon be there.

Things were going well.
Perhaps too well!

But then, suddenly, out of the blue, their good fortune ran out!
Things changed in a split second!
Lady Luck had deserted them!
Disaster had struck!
The look of horror on the children's faces told the story!

Both of them had noticed a strange, orangy-red glow coming from *Murkbog's windows*!
A strange *flickering*, orangy-red glow!
With thick plumes of smoke billowing into the sky from the top of the ruin!

Murkbog Towers was on fire!!!

Chapter 23

The leafy, lawned grounds of Gutbucket Mansion were awash with bright floodlit white, and the grand building itself looking splendidly pink against the night sky, illuminated by spotlights. Rainbow coloured laser beams cut into the blackness and music filled the cool air. Expensive cars...driven by clowns, nurses, Elvis Presleys, lions, witches, pirates, White Rabbits, Kings, Queens, fairies, liquorice allsorts, scarecrows and every other sort of fancy dress you could think of...were pouring down the wide, tree-lined, gravel drive.

Three helicopters had already landed in a meadow and two coaches

had arrived packed with pupils from Snootem School...friends of Honeysuckle and Daffodil. Titania and her daughters, of course, had long since made a run for it in a taxi via a quiet rear exit, aiming to spend the night in a hotel in Leeds before flying to Spain.

Titus Gutbucket, on the other hand, was determined to hold the fort, whilst making some sort of excuse to stop guests from entering the mansion. He was trying to keep his respectability and gain sympathy at the same time! Some sort of triumph out of a complete and utter disaster!

First, he'd hurriedly drunk a few glasses of whisky to drown his sorrows and his anger. Then he'd changed into his spectacular Dracula costume! So now, with Cruncher, as a very life-like gorilla at his side, he was attempting to explain to everyone that the events of the evening were unfortunately cancelled, due to matters beyond his control.

"I'm afraid my wife and daughters have all come down with a dose of dashed chicken pox! Dashed bad luck!" he spouted slightly tipsily to a shivering Lord and Lady Wensleydale, dressed as Tarzan and Jane.

"You mean we can't go indoors, man!" fumed the goose-bumped Lord.

"My wife and I are going to freeze to death out here!"

Just then, a couple dressed as a policeman and a police woman approached the host cloaked in black with his fangs, his dribbling blood, his walking stick and his rubber bat-on-a-spring bouncing round his head...and promptly produced a pair of silver handcuffs!

"Excuse me, sir, but we are arresting you in the name of the law!" burst PC Clegg, putting his hand on Dracula's shoulder. "Anything you may wish to say will be taken down and...!"

"What splendid fancy dresses! What dashed fun!" laughed Dracula drunkenly. "Policeman and woman, eh! I'll show you what I think of the law!"

Then to the utter amazement of all the guests, he stooped forwards and sunk his plastic fangs into WPC Hopkins' neck! The piercing scream that followed silenced the whole, shocked crowd!

The music stopped, and everyone stared open-mouthed at the desperate host, as he lifted his black walking stick and swung it in the air like a baseball bat!

Round and round it went...once, twice, three times...and then...*thwack*!

PC Clegg's helmet sailed through the air, and five hundred pairs of eyes watched as it rose in a great arc and then plummeted into the ornamental pond with a sploshy thud, as it landed on the gas-guzzler's roof, scattering its gaggle of terrified, quacking ducks!

A collective gasp of astonishment gushed from the guests.

They were flabbergasted!

They'd never seen such a performance!

Gutbucket must have taken leave of his senses!

"He's a *real* constable, you know!" came a voice from the crowd, as Lenny and Rita pushed their way to the front in their dancing costumes. "You've had it now, mate! And, can you tell us exactly where our children are? I think we should be leaving with them! You're obviously a complete lunatic!"

Gutbucket, sinking deeper and deeper into the swamp of disgrace by the minute, staggered over to Rita and grabbed her by the waist.

"You wish to dance, madam?" he slobbered.

Lenny, having seen enough, tapped Dracula on the shoulder.

As he turned, Lenny swung his fist...and *thwack*!

Straight on the chin!

Gutbucket bit the dust!

The party was over!

At the back of the chattering crowd, a couple dressed as particularly terrifying tramps...one with a cook's hat perched on her head...headed for their car. The game was over! There would be no launch of the brand new, all-cute, all-rubbish eating, all-talking pet at midnight! They'd failed again!

And gone were all their beautiful thoughts of living in the lap of luxury!

It was back to that dreadful *Murkbog*!

The damp and the draughts, the stone floors and the howling wind. Would their long, miserable days there never end?

Grimmage glumly turned the ignition key and the little car coughed into action.

As it tumbled through the main gates and turned right, he mumbled, "It's those wormsss...those kidsss! I bet they're at the bottom of thisss! One day, I ssswear, I'll have their gutsss for gartersss!"

But little did they know what had happened to their snug little home! If they had done, they would have turned left...

        ...and kept going!

Chapter 24

　　"Quick, we've got to save as many animals as
we can!" yelled Roberta as she dived out of the Rolls, dashed for the
front door and pushed it open.
Maxwell locked the car, making sure the squibbitz couldn't follow.
As they burst into the ruin, they could hardly believe their eyes!
Black, choking smoke filled the downstairs room!
The two piles of sheets by the fireplace were ablaze like small bonfires,
with fountains of swirling sparks fizzing into the air above them.
Boxes of food and clothing were burning wildly, set alight by candles
that had fallen from the swinging candelabra.
Even the wooden table and the three chairs were blazing.
The place was an inferno!
The children put their arms over their faces and pelted across the
room, the flames lapping and licking at their legs. Maxwell, coughing
and spluttering, grabbed the large, rusty water container and doused
the burning sheets, a few of the boxes and one of the chairs. Then he
stamped on one or two of the smaller fires.
Roberta dashed upstairs.
Already, the smoke was creeping around the floor, like thick, black,
writhing serpents.
　　The rat-hogs that had escaped from their cages were gathered
together, cowering in a dark corner, their quills flattened with fear,

whilst the others, trapped in their cages, were howling with fright, along with the captured squibbitz. The two parrots were squawking crazily, flying round and round the room. In another corner were the several larger cages covered with cloths. Robbie had noticed them earlier but hadn't had time to find out what was inside them.

"Maxwell, come up here!" shouted Roberta at the top of her voice. "Help me open all the cages! We've got to get every animal down the spiral staircase!"

Maxwell quickly appeared and together, while still coughing and spluttering, they managed to release all the animals.

"What about the big cages over there!" shouted Maxwell.

"But we've got to move! The smoke's getting thicker and thicker!"

Together they clambered over to the large mystery cages and swept off their cloths.

What they saw next made them freeze with sudden shock!

Inside each cage was a cowering creature, the like of which the children had never seen in their lives!

They stared in amazement as the large animals whined and whimpered.

The creatures were a cross between foxes and badgers!

Fodgers!

FODGER

Like a short, stubby legged, black and white dog, with huge clawed digging paws and a red bushy tail!

They were incredible!

"Quick! We've got to risk it and let them out, and just hope they get on with the rat-hogs and the squibbitz!" shouted Roberta suddenly. "Come on, we've got to get every single animal down to the miners' tunnel!"

During the next frantic few minutes, the children, once again, were like heroic *Pied Pipers*!

The animals seemed to sense their concern and kindness.

They just followed their rescuers with no questions asked!

And soon, every creature was on its way down the long, spiral staircase, leaving the smouldering fires and smoke behind.

As they headed down to the tunnel following Roberta, Maxwell freed the squibbitz in the Rolls and the caravan, and led them through the smoke blackened ruin towards the staircase. The fires were almost out except for the wooden table and the chairs which had suddenly flared up in the draught from the open door.

Everything would soon be destroyed.

Grimmage and Grubbage, when they returned, would have nothing.

At the bottom of the long and winding staircase was the miners' truck, illuminated by a flaming torch, awaiting its next journey. Soon half of the animals had scrambled aboard and were waiting for Maxwell and Roberta to get the show moving!

The other half would run alongside and the parrots would fly.

"What about the Rolls and the caravan?" burst Roberta, just as they were about to start moving the truck. "We can't leave them to Grimmage and Grubbage!"

"No problem!" smiled Maxwell, his face black with soot, and waving the ignition key. "They can't go anywhere! And after all this is over, we'll come back with dad and take 'em home! OK?"

"OK!" replied Roberta with a grin.

Then she looked at all the passengers and the ones by the track, including the six peculiar fodgers.

"Right!" she said gently. "It's time you lot were at home as well! Is everyone ready for the miners' express?"

The squibbitz perked up their ears and looked excited, as though they understood every word. One or two even squeaked the familiar phrases they'd been taught under the school.

"Zziffo, good boy!" squeaked one in particular, jumping up onto Maxwell's shoulder. Maxwell stroked him under his chin. He'd certainly miss his furry mate when he was finally released into the wild, but he knew it was for the best.

The rat-hogs looked a bit anxious, twitching their long rat tails and nibbling one another's quills.

And the fodgers just looked relaxed. Sort of laid back, grooming their bushy red tails and licking their enormous paws.

Slowly, the children began to pump the see-saw up and down,

hoping the truck would begin to move along the rails.

But nothing happened!

They tried again.

Still nothing happened!

"Perhaps there's some kind of brake on!" gasped Maxwell. "Just hang on a sec while I have a look underneath!"

He jumped off and kicked away a wedged-shape chunk of rusty iron on one of the rails that was stopping the wheels from rolling.

But then...as he jumped back on the truck, Roberta suddenly let out a shrill scream that echoed along the tunnel like the whistle of an express train!

Maxwell nearly jumped out of his skin and so did every one of the alarmed animals!

He looked at Roberta, wondering what on earth was the matter.

She was standing on the truck, perfectly still, and pointing to the end of the spiral staircase.

The look on her face was as if she'd just seen a ghost!

Maxwell turned and looked into the warm glow of the torchlight at the bottom of the steps.

And there...silhouetted against the orange...

...were two figures!

Two very familiar figures indeed!!

Chapter 25

"Not ssso fassst, you wormsss!" hissed Grimmage, waving his fists and panting heavily after his dash down the spiral staircase. "You thought you'd get the better of your old headmassster, did you?"

"We'll *still* win! You just watch us, Grimbag!" yelled Roberta defiantly. "You'll *never* get your grubby hands on these animals *again*!"

Maxwell scrambled through all the squibbitz, rat-hogs and fodgers and manned his half of the see-saw. This time when they yanked it up and down, the truck thankfully crept forward. Slowly it picked up speed and rumbled through the tunnel, half the animals running alongside.

Maxwell risked a quick glance behind and saw to his horror, in the distance, the pair of villains climbing aboard the parked trolley.

"Oh, no!! They're coming after us on the other truck!"

"Perhaps...it's all rusted up...and doesn't work...as well...as this one!" gasped Roberta breathlessly, moving up and down on her half of the see-saw.

They rounded the bend and picked up even more speed.

All the running creatures kept up brilliantly!

They'd certainly no intentions of letting Grimmage and Grubbage capture them again!

In next to no time, half-a-dozen blazing torches had whizzed by, and the children released their grips on the see-saw. The wheels slowed down and gradually the truck came to a halt nearly at the last torch. Beyond was the door that led to *The Devil's Back Garden*!

As the rumbling faded away they listened for the other truck.

Was it on its way?

Had Grimmage and Grubbage got it moving?

All seemed quiet, except for the squeaking and chuntering of all the animals which were busily jumping off the trolley, accompanied by the squawking parrots.

Maxwell and Roberta jogged towards the door.

The creatures followed.

There was no time to lose.

They *had* to get them all to safety and then get back and deal with the enemy!

As the door swung open, the children led the horde of joyful animals into the chilly air and back into their own amazing wilderness.

It was nearly midnight and the cloudless sky was jet black, scattered with twinkling stars, like black velvet sprinkled with diamonds.

Holding it up were all the tall chimneys, some fat, some thin, but all still pouring out their poisons into the air. The power station, the sewage works, and the re-cycling plant never stopped. Even rubbish kept pouring into the tip all through the night, making the mountain higher and higher.

The motorways that made the traingle's walls had fallen quiet. Just the headlight beams of the odd sleepless lorry or car could be seen gliding along the ramparts. Tomorrow the roads would be full of traffic again, pumping out their gases.

But the children knew that it was home and freedom for the squibbitz, the rat-hogs and the fodgers. They'd lived and thrived on the junk, and somehow, over the years, they'd been created from squirrels and rabbits, rats and hedgehogs and foxes and badgers. Some strange, unknown mutations had taken place, probably due to the toxins in the air, soil and water. Perhaps even more new species existed that had been lucky enough not to fall prey to Grimmage and Grubbage.

Who knows? But for the moment the children were just happy to leave these particular ones in peace.

Soon most of the released animals had vanished into the murky depths of the dead or dying vegetation.

Many disappeared down holes and vanished into cracks in the stacks of junk.

Maxwell and Roberta had mixed feelings, of course.

They'd enjoyed looking after the squibbitz for the last three months...feeding them, exercising them, playing with them...but they knew they would be happier here than being cooped up in the school-house.

They certainly seemed happy enough!

Zziffo jumped onto Maxwell's shoulder and licked his ear.

"Me good boy! Me Zziffo!" he squeaked.

Maxwell tickled him under his chin.

He'd definitely miss *him*.

The squibbit jumped down onto the ground, gave one last look up at Maxwell and Roberta and vanished into the night.

The children looked at one another with tears in their eyes.

"Come on, let's just destroy as many cage-traps as we can find," said Roberta quietly, both sad and happy at once, "and then I think we'd better get home! Lenny and Rita'll be having kittens, as usual. They've probably called the pol...!"

Suddenly, the sound of a door slamming behind them, made them both spin round and look towards the entrance. And there, standing in the shadowy starlight in front of the closed door, were none other than Grimmage and Grubbage.

"You wormsss!!" screeched Grimmage. "Where are they all? What have you done with them?"

"They've *gone*! Gone *forever*!" yelled Roberta, through her tears.

"You'll *never* get your hands on one *again*!" shouted Maxwell.

"We'll see to that!"

"I've worked for yearsss and yearsss to make my fortune with 'the perfect pet'!" growled Grimmage, his voice menacingly quiet.

"And now you two nuisances think that we're finished, do you?" chipped in Grubbage, wringing her chubby hands. "Well, you can think again!"

The two rogues stepped forwards.

Maxwell and Roberta stepped backwards, wondering what was coming next!

All at once, Grimmage and Grubbage darted off through a tangle of dead branches...to the fallen, rotten tree trunk next to the black, stinking bog of oozing mud.

"We'll jussst grab thisss little fellow as a keep sssake!" hissed Grimmage, reaching over the dead bough.

Grubbage jumped onto the dead wood and helped Grimmage lift the cage with the trapped rat-hog he'd introduced to the children earlier.

"Oh no you won't!" yelled Maxwell. "Let it go...*now*!"

But Grimmage lifted the cage higher and higher until it was above his head, like a victorious football captain holding aloft a trophy at a cup-final.

"Not on your life, you worm!" crowed Grimmage. "This one will do for the time being! Until we return!"

"Let it go!" ordered Roberta. "You'll never re...!"

Just then, with a crackling crunch, Grubbage's foot went through the rotten wood of the fallen tree!

She overbalanced...toppled off the bough...collided with Grimmage... and to the sheer horror of both of them...

...they tumbled backwards...

...into the oozing mass of black, stinking mud...

The cage with the rat-hog was catapulted out of Grimmage's grip...flew through the air...and landed, to the utter delight of the rat-hog, in Maxwell's outstretched arms with a soft thud!

Meanwhile, on the other side of the fallen, rotten tree trunk...things were getting a bit sticky!

In fact, a lot sticky!

Grimmage and Grubbage were sinking!

Fast!

Already the black, stinking mud had reached their chests!

"It's all *your* fault, woman!" snapped Grimmage, helpless to resist the pull of the oozy, bottomless bog.

"I should never have got mixed up with you in the first place!" snapped back Grubbage. "I knew it would end with us up to our necks in...!"

The mud reached their chins...

       ...then their mouths...

...then their noses!

Then they vanished altogether...amid a gurgle of belching, black slime...

       A few fat bubbles broke on the surface...and then the bog returned to its normal tranquil self as though nothing had ever happened!

It had swallowed its victims.

Grimmage and Grubbage had gone...*forever*!

Maxwell and Roberta looked at one another with anxious faces.

They'd witnessed the grizzly end of their two arch enemies.

A particularly grim and grubby end!

Should they have helped?

Thrown a branch?

Lent a hand?

       Silently they opened the rat-hog's cage and let him bound to freedom. In a couple of seconds he'd disappeared and joined his mates.

Maxwell and Roberta headed back to the tunnel, took one last glance at *The Forbidden Triangle* under the night sky and closed the door on the amazingly weird but wonderful wilderness.

Then they walked past the miners' trucks, with the parrots on their shoulders, along the passageway under the school and up through the trap door onto the stage in the hall. They quickly put the parrots in the school-house and headed to their classroom. The clock said that it was just ten minutes to midnight.

"Wonder how the '*do*' of the century went?" whispered Roberta with a smile, as they crept out of the classroom door and onto the playground.

"Hope Honey and Daff enjoy their birthday!" said Maxwell, with a grin on his face.

And with that, the two of them, walking hand-in-hand under the stars, headed for home...no doubt having to face the music, yet again, when they got there!!

Their great adventure with the squibbitz was over!

They would never, ever see them again!

Or, would they?

Squibbitz-3
by James David

In the last of the trilogy about
the weird world beneath Chestnut Hill Juniors,
Maxwell and Roberta find themselves
deep in another adventure with the strange
creatures that live down below!
It's a hot summer in Kirkthwaite...
the Squibbitz & their friends begin
to explore the town causing more
than a few problems!
Titus Gutbucket decides to step in...
to clear his name and pay his debts!
Plus great surprises from Lenny and Rita,
and Miss Teezil!
Will Ozzie & Robbie get dragged into
a TV dance show?
And did Grimmage and Grubbage really
come to a sticky end in Part Two?

Find out in the comic last part of the
SQUIBBITZ!!

Published 2009

Watch out for more from Chestnut Hill!

-a spin-off series from 'The Squibbitz'-

Meet Maxwell and Roberta again in

Tales from Chestnut Hill Juniors

by James David

Two short stories in each book
featuring
Maxwell & Roberta
and the other children
in Miss Teezil's class!

&

PUZZLES and QUIZZES
about the tales!!

Book No. 1 with 2 stories:-

THE MAGIC BIKE !
and
CONKERS !

Published 2009

MAGIC BENEATH THE MOORS!!

At 3 o'clock in the middle of the night,
a mysterious green glow beckons Tom
from his bedroom!
He makes a fantastic, magical discovery
and his life will never be the same again!

Join Tom on his amazing adventures
with his brilliant new secret power!!

ORDER DIRECT FROM THE PUBLISHERS
dedicated & signed First Editions
all titles £6.99, post free

AQUA CRYSTA Series

Part 1 - **Next to No Time**
dedicated to ....

Part 2 - **Deeper Than Yesterday**
dedicated to ....

Part 3 - **Forever Crystal**
dedicated to ....

Part 4 - **StoneSpell**
dedicated to ....

Complete 4-part First Series £24 inc. p&p
dedicated to ....

Part 5 - **The Ammonite Seekers** [Published 2009]
dedicated to ....

SQUIBBITZ – 1
dedicated to ....

SQUIBBITZ – 2
dedicated to ....

SQUIBBITZ – 3 [Published 2009]
dedicated to ....

Complete series (available 2009) **£18** inc. p&p

REMOTE CONTROL Pt. 1
dedicated to ....

Name ....

Address ....

.... Postcode ....

cheques only – 'Moonbeam Publishing'
send order form to:- Moonbeam Publishing, PO Box 100,
Whitby, North Yorkshire, YO22 5WA

or order online:- www.aquacrysta.com
Tel: 01947 811703   Email: moonbeampublishing@yahoo.co.uk